Antonion Borges's far-ranging curiosity and inventiveness belie his formal training. Having graduated from the Massachusetts Eye and Ear Infirmary Department of Harvard Medical School as well as the Sawyer School in Radio and Television Broadcasting, he works in the field of ophthalmology and pathology. His books testify to the truth that he is a modern version of the Renaissance Man.

Dedication

For Peter A. Koch, 1949-2015, for his great influence in helping and reaching out to many people from all walks of life with his kind spirit, and for assisting the world community in honor of his late father.

For Ultimate Warrior, James Brian Hellwig, 1959-2014, the philosopher who gave the strongest speech of his lifetime and one for the ages when he said, "Every man's heart one day beats its final beat. His lungs breathe their final breath. And if what that man did in his life makes the blood pulse through the bodies of others and makes them bleed deeper in something larger than life, then his essence, his spirit, will be immortalized by the storytellers, by the loyalty, by the memory of those who honor him and make the running the man did live forever!"

Antonion Borges

Annihilation of a Planet II

Alpha … Omega

AUSTIN MACAULEY PUBLISHERS™
LONDON · CAMBRIDGE · NEW YORK · SHARJAH

Copyright © Antonion Borges (2017)

The right of Antonion Borges to be identified as author of this has been asserted by him in accordance with section 77 and 78 of the Copyright, Designs and Patents Act 1988.

All rights reserved. No part of this publication may be reproduced, stored in a retrieval system, or transmitted in any form or by any means, electronic, mechanical, photocopying, recording, or otherwise, without the prior permission of the publishers.

Any person who commits any unauthorized act in relation to this publication may be liable to criminal prosecution and civil claims for damages.

A CIP catalogue record for this title is available from the British Library.

ISBN 9781786933942 (Paperback)
ISBN 9781786933959 (Hardback)
ISBN 9781786933966 (E-Book)
www.austinmacauley.com

First Published (2018)
Austin Macauley Publishers Ltd™
25 Canada Square
Canary Wharf
London
E14 5LQ

Acknowledgments

I gratefully acknowledge the help I have received from my family and friends throughout the world.

Additional thanks to Sharon Reynolds, who patiently typed a great portion of the chapters from my handwritten tablets.

I owe special gratitude to my editor, Drollene P. Brown, who has been my counsel and inspiration as I wrote a novel that will stand through the end of time.

Introduction
Life and Time

Life and Time once lived peacefully together. Life blossomed with creatures great and small; awash with great oceans, Life was filled with rolling hills that met the vast blue sky in the far horizon. Then Man came into Life; it was he who calculated Time for his own benefit, not knowing the ramifications. Man began to use Time to plan his existence and survival in agriculture and other strategies for his future. Slowly Time gained the power over Life ... and sentenced Life to death. Hungry with its new supremacy over Life, Time became the master, controlling all Life as it came into existence. Time forgot—refused to remember—its peaceful nirvana together with Life before the arrival of Man.

But in the end, Life will prevail and put an end to Time. For Time will eventually realize its existence came from Life.

1
This is Progress?

Seagulls cloy the sky high above the beach, their wingspans outstretched like flying kites in the bright sunlight. White, feathered cirrus clouds spread out against the blue heaven, as the sun kisses the multi-ripples of waves below on the ocean surface, glowing and sparkling on a hot day.

Just so the sea of Time rolls in the soft undulation of waves toward the coast as it picks up speed, a mighty wave crashing into boulders on shore, shooting the sparkling water upward like a geyser. Other parts of the wave gently roll onto the sandy beach, glistening on the wet sand. The wind of Time swirls and dashes in where the sea of Time left behind its mark, blowing debris of sand and leaves and twigs in a circular pattern into the near grounds and roads, as the sea did. As the detritus comes up against a building, a second wind scatters it all in every direction, and the debris goes in many different places.

Annihilation of a Planet II

Like the sea of Time and the wind of Time, men and women of a different time now stand to walk the earth.

In the year 2251 a man gazed out a window, following the course of a leaf flying before the wind. He was Paul Linsdale, son of the late, renowned Simon Linsdale, whose Omega Starr project failed when the androids on Mars severed the relationship between Man and Machine; the androids, called Cybernauts, had decided to become their own masters and to disobey mankind's Starr Project ambitions on the red planet.

As Paul watched the leaves being whisked across his grand airgell window—composed of 98% condensed air—and followed the seagulls in their flight across the sky, he said aloud, "It is true. We are only sand in the wind. The sand of Time is constantly moving, carried by the sea and the wind, and no one lives forever." He pounded his right fist into his left hand. "But one's legacy can! I must send an expedition team to bring Lawrence back to earth. That will be my American legacy, and it will honor my father's name."

Paul thought about Lawrence's acts as a world hero when he single-handedly planted the mega bomb on the androids' space craft to be detonated after leaving the red planet, annihilating the ship and all 900 crew members into fragments of space debris.

Stalking over to the console, Linsdale spoke firmly, "Computer, dial NASA."

In a few moments an image of a man appeared on the screen. "Professor Paul, how are you?"

"I'm fine, thank you!"

"How can I help you, professor?"

"I'd like to send a manned mission to Mars to bring Lawrence Android B12 back to earth."

Ortiz, the man speaking from the large screen, asked, "Permission to step in?"

"Permission granted."

The professor continued to look at the screen as Ortiz stepped out in a virtual image and looked around the lab. "Nice picture of the missus! I couldn't see it from the flat screen." Ortiz's holograph picked up the picture, looking at a beautiful, smiling blonde in a short dress. He set the picture down carefully on the redwood desk. "*Ott mi*! Some guys are just born lucky."

Paul nodded his head in agreement, looking at Ortiz with a wide smile.

"Back to your request," Ortiz said. "That's going to be difficult to do."

"Why?" Paul asked as he sank into his chair, his knuckles white as he gripped the edge of his desk.

"It will be difficult to get financial backing again from all the sovereign countries that funded the last expedition to Mars. It is being called the big blunder dome operation by the public. We've gotten a bad rep from that failed mission. Don't you realize that? This is the complication we now face. It's been hard

Annihilation of a Planet II

for NASA to get even small missions approved by the board for funding."

Ortiz picked up a china vase, turning it 'round and 'round in his hands.

"Be careful with that," Paul said nervously. "It's from the Ming dynasty and probably worth your life's savings. It's more than 880 years old."

Gently putting the vase back down on its protective case, Ortiz hunched his shoulders. "Wow! I had no idea a vase could be that valuable!" Throwing down a quarter-sized coin, Ortiz watched as it made contact with the floor and instantly turned into a virtual chair. He sat facing the professor. As he leaned back, his image began to fluctuate for a few seconds while he adjusted to the chair, and then his image became solid again.

"Continue, professor," Ortiz said as soon as he was settled. "Why and how will we benefit from retrieving Lawrence? Enlighten me."

"Well, for one thing, I found an old disc of my father's showing the blueprint matrix of Lawrence's inner ability. He is capable of placing data entry of the terrain of Mars and its atmosphere into his artificial pineal gland, his third eye, which never closes. It is always active, taking in unbelievable information for the 29 years he's been there—hoisted, as he is, on the death pole—collecting the important data on Mars, day and night, even through sandstorms, without damage. We cannot sit back and allow this information to get into the wrong hands. That is why time is of the essence!"

"What he has, we know already, the climate, soil readings, the—"

"No!" Paul interrupted. "There is more! A lot more." He wiped perspiration from his forehead. "Before he blew up the traitorous Cybernauts' spacecraft, Lawrence and the other androids found an alien space camp on Mars. It pre-dates our history here on Earth. My father was able to retrieve that information from Lawrence before the humanoid was hanged on the pole and lost contact. It showed that the aliens who built the space camp came from the asteroid belt that was once a planet between Mars and Jupiter. Apparently these aliens had made poor decisions regarding energy for sustaining their people. They literally destroyed their own planet. All that is left are fragments that orbit around the area where once it was a thriving planet, full of life. A great portion of the fragments of the planet rained into Jupiter's stormy clouds, disappearing forever. Other fragments collided with Mars, developing huge craters that—"

"That could have damaged Mars' electromagnetic field," Ortiz blurted, interrupting the professor. "That would have led to more damage occurring slowly, over time. That means—"

"That Mars's atmosphere vanished ... vanquished," Linsdale said, finishing Ortiz's sentence. "The ocean slowly evaporated, and the Martian landscape became dry, baked and barren. Some of the fragments made it into our orbit, creating craters on the moon, giving us the famous profile of the man in the moon. And in theory that

Annihilation of a Planet II

could have been the six-mile wide asteroid that struck the earth 66 million years ago near Chicxulub, Mexico, which ended the age of the dinosaurs as far as our knowledge goes."

Ortiz's look of astonishment encouraged Linsdale to go on.

"I have a hypothesis that some of the fragments of the planet even made their way to the Kuiper belt beyond Neptune's orbit. The question that now remains is whether Pluto is the core of the annihilated planet; its trajectory would have spun away into an elliptical orbit, taking five large asteroids as its moons. All the other planets are aligned around the sun in their respective orbits channeling around the sun like a sundial. This anomaly that is Pluto would have given birth to Halley's comet."

"Professor, this is exciting stuff. Lots of new studies for us!"

"Um-hm," Paul said, beginning to pace. "I wonder with whom they were at war. Was it technology that went against them as we saw 30 years ago when the Cybernauts my father created turned against us? You can rest assured I will not make that same mistake." He shook his head. "Knowing my father as I did, I strongly believe someone sabotaged his mission. I suspect a scientist by the name of Rick Javens, who loved to throw his weight around at the lab, ordering people here and there when I played there as a kid. He was found dead with my father, who had two gunshot wounds to his chest."

"Your hunch is right," Ortiz confessed. "Later on the day we found your father, we found a hidden camera that had recorded everything that happened. Javens had, indeed, sabotaged the Cybernauts to cause them to go rogue. Your father confronted Javens, who fired the shots. Before your dad died, he injected his killer with a toxic chemical to his neck."

Paul gasped when he heard the truth of what had happened that day long ago. It had been kept from him all these years. His hand went to his mouth as his eyes welled with tears.

"Are you okay, Dr. Linsdale?" Ortiz asked.

"Yes."

Ortiz put a hand on Paul's shoulder. "I know this must be hard on you, but we had to keep this top secret, away from the media."

Linsdale nodded and regained his composure. "Let's get back to our discussion."

"Right. Surely bad energy decisions didn't completely destroy that planet," Ortiz said, skepticism showing on his face.

"There are records of nuclear warfare that brought famine. Scores of people died of starvation. Others knowingly drank water polluted by radiation. They knew they would die within a week's time, but they were so thirsty they drank it anyway. The radiation was immense in the air and the sea. There was no place to escape it … except for the camp on Mars. The old planet was doomed for destruction by sunlight, which served as a lightning wick that

Annihilation of a Planet II

ignited it to oblivion. We must learn from those Mars aliens so we won't make the mistakes they made."

Ortiz unfolded himself from the chair with only a slight amount of static. "I'll organize a meeting of the International Board for Climate and Planetary Science immediately and have a seat there for you. Can you make it in three days?"

"Yes. No problem," Linsdale said in a calm voice.

"One more thing, professor."

Paul looked at Ortiz.

"We might have to auction that 880-year-old vase to help raise the money for the mission, if you don't mind."

Paul clinched his teeth together, then nodded his head in agreement. "Ortiz, you scoundrel. You got me, then."

"Great! I'll get in touch with a licensed broker. I'm hoping that should cover a lot of this project's cost."

"I'm sure it will," Paul muttered as Ortiz walked back to the large screen on the wall, touched it and was automatically absorbed back into it. His flat image looked at Paul again.

"Did you forget something?" Paul asked, his eyes turning toward the chair Ortiz had left behind.

"Oh, sorry!" From his wrist watch Ortiz deactivated the virtual chair, and the image disappeared from Paul's office. "Okay. Goodbye, professor. See you in three days!"

Ortiz's image began to fade, then it suddenly came back full force on the screen. "And keep in mind, professor, no holding back any more information. We have to work together."

The screen faded to black but only for an instant. In place of Ortiz on the screen was the image of Lawrence tied onto the death pole.

"Bringing you home, old friend," Paul said.

Paul's new vehicle, a Chrysler sealander, pulled up to the office to take him home. "How was your day, professor?" the vehicle asked.

"It was exhausting."

"Home, sir?"

"Yes, home." He stretched back on the sealander's recliner for a quick nap as the sounds of a Mozart composition flowed through the speakers. Paul's eyes closed, and a relaxing smile crossed his face. A voice came through the speakers, interrupting his nap and turning off the music.

"Hi, honey. I see you're on your way back."

Paul sat up quickly. "How did you know I was heading home?"

"Your new sealander sent me a text to inform me, to give me ample time to get rid of my boyfriend before you arrived." She giggled. "Just kidding, honey!"

"Very funny."

"You don't mind stopping at our local store and getting me some red tomatoes, do you? I'm making my secret tomato sauce you like for pasta tonight. Oh, and get a bottle of reds ... um, red wine."

"Eliven, can't you have our homecare android ... uh, Drika, isn't it ... do it?"

"She's out walking the dogs."

Paul sighed. "Okay. I'll do it. No problem."

He shut his eyes. He appreciated the fact that his wife, Eliven, still cooked meals for him the old fashioned way. It was sweet and sexy at the same time. However, there were two things he had to do right away. He had to get a second homecare android for Eliven, and he had to reprogram his sealander.

Paul pressed a button and talked to his new vehicle in a stern voice. "From now on, I will inform my wife that I'm coming home. Can't a man have some little privacy in relating to his wife? Is that too much to ask?"

"Sorry," the sealander replied. "That was a default program. I won't do that again, professor."

"Thank you." Paul reclined again, his eyes closed, as he listened to Mozart with a smile.

The sealander picked up speed, going more than 100 mph on the light energy from the Tesla road belt that elevated the car and lifted it three inches from the belt, eliminating the need for tires. As the music filled the space in which Paul reclined, his mind wandered unbidden to the mechanics that allowed his vehicle to glide so effortlessly and rapidly. The ground state electrons from the S orbital coming from the Tesla belt road were rising high in energy as the opposite electrons spun from the sealander to give it lift. The D orbital was being controlled by pitch oscillation energy waves from the sealander, while sound frequency worked to accelerate the control of speed for the vehicle.

Paul smiled as he thought of Nikola Tesla, whose inventions were not as appreciated in his lifetime as much as they were centuries later. He raised a shot glass of vodka in tribute to Tesla, who said about the scientists of his time, "The present is theirs. The future, for which I have really worked, is mine."

The sealander's amphibious nature was equally as interesting. When the vehicle dove underwater, the radiators at the front of the car's grill would siphon the water like a fish's gill would do, at the same time producing oxygen inside the passenger compartment. For emergencies, there was on every sealander an oxygen tank and an automatic floatation device to cause the vehicle to resurface and allow the car to work as a motorboat.

Paul's sealander passed similar vehicles, all of them using a method of traveling conceived by Tesla when he placed a long line of lights in the ground that could be charged miles away from a generator, eliminating the use of fossil fuel. This line, or Tesla belt, prevented snow-covered roads by immediately melting the snowflakes as they made contact, saving cities in the Snow Belt section of the country millions of dollars a year in snow-plowing during its winter months. Some of the obsolete snow-blowing trucks were preserved in museums across the region.

In twenty minutes Linsdale's sealander stopped in front of a supermarket. "We have arrived, professor."

Paul awoke as the recliner moved forward. He stretched his arms. "Ahh! I feel refreshed."

A beautiful female child android walked out to the sealander. "What may I get you from the market?" she asked. "I'm here to get your order and do the shopping for your convenience."

"No need. I'm good. I will go in myself. I need to stretch my legs from this long ride." The ride of 20 minutes would have been considered short two centuries earlier. Time had collapsed in an era when everything moved faster and more efficiently than ever before. Paul looked at the little android as he stepped out of the sealander. "What model are you?"

"I'm a B3," she said, smiling, as they walked along together.

"I remember that model," Paul said. "It was one of the robotics I designed when I was a freshman in college, some 19 years ago."

The android smiled. "Enjoy your shopping!" She sat down with other B3s who were waiting to help the next human shoppers find what they needed.

Linsdale walked into the market as the airgell door slid open. He was immediately confronted by a bearded old man. White, wiry hair straggled down around his face.

Antonion Borges

"Can you spare a bit?" he asked. "I haven't eaten in days."

Trying not to grimace at the man's body odor, Paul looked at the bedraggled old fellow and gave him a coin.

"Ahh! A right shiny one, this! Blessa sir!" His smile revealed yellow, decayed teeth, but only for an instant. Holding the gift like a treasure, he shuffled off into the market to buy something to eat, cackling with glee as he hobbled down the aisles.

Paul whispered to himself. "Humanity! Where is it going in the 23rd century? We were making such great progress by the mid-21st century until greed and power unsettled everything again. At least that's so if I can believe what I read in Dad's collection of old *Time Life* magazines."

He strolled past androids selecting food from the shelves for their customers, who waited in their sealanders in the parking lot listening to music, reading, napping or gossiping with occupants of nearby vehicles. A long robotic arm from the overhead ceiling moved downward to a pallet that had canned goods, moving one can at a time and placing it neatly on the shelves with the labels perfectly facing for proper display. One B3 asked the robotic arm for chicken soup, which was out of her reach on a top shelf. The arm stopped stacking the shelves and gently picked up the desired item, placing it in the B3's cart next to foodstuffs she had already selected. The robotic arm then went back to stocking the shelves. Every three aisles had a robotic arm working away.

Annihilation of a Planet II

A voice came on the loudspeaker as Paul was ambling with his cart along the vegetable aisle. "Just in for our human shoppers—fresh ears of corn and potatoes from our heartland, U.S.A., for only 99 cents a pound." Paul looked around the vegetable section seeing androids and people shopping together. Human children were there, too, making silly faces, smirking at one another.

"Mom, Sammy is giving me those googly eyes again and sticking out his tongue at me."

Sammy, a pale-faced boy with blue eyes and blond hair, looked up at his mom, looking as though he were wondering what she would say. She seemed upset.

"Now Sammy, did I not tell you to stop teasing your little sister? If you keep doing that, I'm taking away your game board!"

"Geeze," the little sister said. She obviously knew how cute she was, her hair in pigtails and freckles sprinkling over her face. She was completely in control. "We are not going to put up with this bad behavior, Sammy!" the child said, clearly mimicking words she'd heard her mother say.

The poor little boy looked at Paul with a desperate expression, walking away with his mother and sister, as if the world would come to an end for him without his game board.

Paul shook his head and grinned as he picked up some tomatoes, pressed them lightly and smelled them at the stem to make sure they were fresh. After bagging the chosen ones, he noticed other tomatoes on the shelf and felt them all around. He didn't bother to smell them. With a disgusted look on his face, he muttered, "These robots must be sleeping on the job." He walked to the liquor aisle and picked up a Merlot. On the label were the words, "A Taste of Mars."

The words brought Lawrence to the front of Paul's mind. *Soon my friend, soon,* he thought. *I hope to convince the board members to bring you back home.*

Paul approached the register, where a couple of kids were working. The girl was operating the register by pressing a button that moved the small conveyer belt along. An infrared light automatically rang up each item without the clerk having to pick them up. As the last item went through, the total of the purchase glowed on the clerk's monitor.

"That's $22.03, please," she said with a smile. Paul swiped his card as the teenage boy was bagging the purchased groceries. Such jobs were always given to young people to help teach them work ethics.

B3s did not go through the checkout lines, and Paul looked around to make sure no humans were around to get in line behind him. He was curious about the young people who were working, and he figured a conversation wouldn't hold up anyone.

"What are your ambitions in life?" he asked.

"I'm going to be a veterinarian," the girl said.

"That's a terrific field," Paul said, smiling broadly. "Animals are wonderful to be around, and helping them is a marvelous occupation."

"Pets help humans, too," she said, her eyes shining. "Having a dog brought my grandma's blood pressure down."

"Animals are God's creatures, just as humans are," Paul said, nodding his head. "I can see your chosen profession will enable you to make a great contribution to the world."

Tilting his head, Paul turned to the boy. "And you, young man?"

"I intend to join the military, sir, to pilot drones into enemy territory in the effort to eliminate drug warlords."

"Excellent choice!" Paul declared. "This is an important field, one that benefits mankind. It is imperative that we stay on top and above our created counterparts, the androids. If we weaken, and if they see we can no longer think clearly to invent and run the world correctly due to being high on drugs, they will calculate us out of the equation. They will contrive to lead, and we may become enslaved to them. That's the horror we now face with the rise of these machines. We must always be alert and drug-free 24/7 around them. We now live in perilous times. The machines seem to be waiting for the chance to take over."

Paul noticed the girl's eyes, wide with dismay. They boy looked grim. "Well," Paul said, clearing his throat, "enough of that. I have to go. Have a great day, kids!" He smiled and waved at the two youngsters as he made his way to the front, where the sealander was moving out of its parking spot and pulling around to pick up Paul. The vehicle door opened upward, and the chair extended outward from the sealander. Paul sat on the chair with his groceries on his lap, and the chair slowly receded into the sealander. There was plenty of headroom, and he didn't have to tuck his head down. He placed the bag next to him as the sealander drove off the lot and onto the Tesla belt. In two seconds flat it was going 100 mph.

Paul thought about his conversation with the two promising young people. He thought about how technical progress had made some occupations obsolete. Police work had certainly changed over the decades. Because of the Tesla belt system, there was never a speeding ticket to be written, and no one was ever pulled over for DUI. Anyone could get into his sealander drunk and get safely home. There were no car accidents, so no reason for liability car insurance. Many insurance companies had gone out of business.

Professor Linsdale's estate was surrounded by a lake, into which the sealander smoothly submerged. A few minutes later it propelled itself to the surface of the lake and floated like a boat, propelling itself onto the dry dock. The door hatch lifted open, and the car seat pivoted out with the professor holding his groceries.

"Have a good evening, professor," the sealander said, as the seat pivoted back in and the door closed.

Annihilation of a Planet II

Paul walked across the dock without a backward glance at the sealander, which would be waiting there for him the following morning. As he walked onto the large veranda of his home, double doors opened for him.

"Hi, honey!" Eliven kissed him on the lips. "Hmm? Rough day, I see. Your lips feel tight and tense." Stepping back, she looked at his tired face and gave him a worried look.

"You can say that again," Paul said.

"Thanks for getting the tomatoes."

"In a way I'm glad I did. I met and talked to two young people. The youth of today hold our future in their hands."

Taking the tomatoes from Paul, Eli gave his shoulder a squeeze and walked into the kitchen, where she had various bowls and dishes holding her grandmother's secret spices and other ingredients that would go into the sauce. After washing the tomatoes, she placed them on a cutting board and diced them into small pieces before sliding them from the board into a pan that began to heat on the countertop when Eli pushed a button. As the tomatoes began to sizzle, she added the waiting ingredients.

Paul walked into the kitchen with the bottle of wine. Opening a cabinet drawer, he pulled out a cork opener and peeled off the seal on the bottle. As he twisted the cork opener into the cork, Eli took up the conversation as though there had never been a pause.

"Oh, a happy bunch of kids, I take it?"

"Yes, they were," he said with a smile.

As Eli set the timer to go off when the sauce was ready, Paul popped open the wine bottle. He poured two glasses of the wine and handed one to his wife. They walked into the living room together.

Taking a few sips of the wine and beginning to feel relaxed, he took her by the waist and kissed her again, this time with passion.

Her eyes sparkled open, then closed, feeling the kiss she had been looking for when Paul first entered the house. She pulled back. "Now, Paul, *that* was a kiss."

The two plopped down on the sofa. Eli brushed her long blond hair back away from her face, took a sip from her wine, and then placed it on a glass table in front of them.

"Honey, when are we going to have children to run around in this big house?" she asked.

"I can't seem to think of any reason for delaying anymore," he said, looking into her eyes. "My time-consuming projects are done, so I'll have time to be a dad."

She squeezed his hand, knowing he was thinking about his own childhood, seldom seeing his father because of Simon's obsession with his lab work.

"I'm a full professor now," Paul continued, "so our money worries are over." He looked deeply into her eyes. "I think we should start right away."

Annihilation of a Planet II

As he placed his wine glass near hers on the table, he gently leaned toward her and whispered in her ear, "How about a little dessert before dinner?"

2
Let's Make a Deal.

The International Board for Climate and Planetary Science convened with members from all over the world sitting around a big, round table. It was polished to such a shine that each person's reflection showed in the mahogany finish. There were 30 members seated at the table. In chairs against the wall, Paul Linsdale and two other people sat with papers in their hands. Screens around the room showed the presence of scientists, engineers and politicians from around the world. NASA personnel were represented on one screen, and three members of the International Monetary Fund were in attendance on another screen. No reporters were allowed, because one of the topics was classified. Each person in attendance, either present or online, had top secret clearance.

A man stood at the table and looked at the screens positioned around the room. "Ladies and gentlemen, I am Martin Goodwill, and I am Chairman of the

International Board of Climate and Planetary Science. You, who are observers, are here because of extraordinary circumstance. Although some of what we say here must be kept secret from the rest of the world, you have reason to know what is said here—some of you on a need-to-know basis. We are here today at the request of Dr. Paul Linsdale and Dr. George Stevens, two men with inspiring ideas that have helped change the world as we know it. It is with great pleasure that I first call on Dr. Stevens to introduce his project."

The members of the board applauded as Stevens stood and made his way to the podium. He smiled and said, "Thank you for the warm response." He paused until the applause died down. "Our unmanned deep-sea subs have found new, unexplored ocean floors near the islands off Cape Verde—stacks of pillar rocks that give rise and birth to some of our deadly hurricanes. As everyone is aware, when the water current moves on the great ocean conveyor belt around such stacks of mountainous rocks, a hurricane is slowly forming, swirling around like a spoon mixing your coffee from your hand's rotation."

Stevens looked over at his research partner, a dark-haired woman wearing wireless glasses, and nodded. "We call this the coffee spoon theory," he said, smiling, "but in this case it's the ocean current's energy swirling the water around these large stacks of stones, rather than your hand on the end of a spoon." He paused for the laughter that rippled across the audience.

"Now most of these small hurricanes will die out as quickly as they form during hurricane season," George continued, "but some will grow with rapid, swirling velocity as the earth's core of gravitational pull gives them strength and power. A storm like this can slowly make its way to the various Atlantic coastlines, injuring or killing anything in its wake with its high winds damaging homes and businesses. We can stop such hurricanes by destroying these stacks of pillared rocks with specialized deep-sea subs using cold fusion lasers. These lasers will blast the boulders into small piles of rock that will scatter along the sea bed, no longer posing a threat for producing hurricanes."

A murmur of surprise rolled around the table and was silently mimed on the screens. People were looking at each other in wonder.

"We're looking to build ten of these subs," Stevens declared, "and that is why I am here today."

"What is the cost? How much money do you seek for this project?" a board member asked.

"We need $1.3 billion to fund this project, to design and build the subs."

There was a collective gasp, but the board members began to whisper among themselves. They compared the notes they had made on the pre-printed project declaration presented to them beforehand. Heads nodded, and Goodwill stepped to the podium next to Stevens. "Do the members of the board agree to Dr. Stevens' proposal?"

Annihilation of a Planet II

A woman got up from her chair, turned to whisper to two other members, and then came forward, joining Goodwill and Stevens. "It's official. Project Cold Fusion is a go!"

She shook hands with the two men at the podium and returned to her chair amid applause from the members; a glance at the screen showed the silent listeners applauding, too. Stevens said thank you to the board members. He waved to the distant audiences before taking his seat, at ease now that his presentation was over and his project approved.

Goodwill spoke again. "Now I take great pride in introducing Dr. Paul Linsdale, who has taken over the work of his late father, Dr. Simon Linsdale. The work of these two men has revolutionized our way of life, from the sealander and the Tesla belts it glides over to our humanoid robots that do all our heavy to simple daily work. All these inventions have made our lives more productive and allowed our family lives to be fuller, with more quality time."

Applause broke out, and Goodwill held up his hand. "It is well that you show your appreciation for the Linsdales' work. Your virtual self can now go anywhere in the world or even take a jog or walk in the park with a friend while your physical self remains in the comfort of your home. Just the other day I was able to attend my grandmother's funeral in Austria. I had to be somewhere else too close to the time to actually go there, but I went anyway, wearing a suit and tie, looking down at her beloved face for the last time." He paused to wipe a tear from his eye.

"These portals are costly," Goodwill said, "but they are worth every dollar, and I tell you this for a fact. On that note, ladies and gentlemen, I give you Dr. Paul Linsdale."

The board room exploded with applause as Paul stepped up to the podium and shook hands with Goodwill. "Thank you for that introduction, Martin," Paul said, as the applause began to die down.

"People, we have a problem ... or as they said back in the 20th century, 'Houston, we have a problem.'" Paul turned to make eye contact with Ortiz, who was sitting with the other members of the board. Ortiz nodded and tapped his copy of the proposal that had been handed to every board member that morning.

Paul steadied himself, knowing he had to get this right. How could he make them see that Lawrence had to be brought home? "As you know, my father built Lawrence"—people around the table nodded—"Lawrence, who is decaying on the death pole on the surface of Mars, and who has been collecting crucial scientific data for nearly three decades. Two weeks ago the beacon signal went dead."

A blonde from Denmark stood up and asked, "What data have been collected, and why is this matter so crucial? Why do we need the data?"

Paul smiled and replied, "I'm glad you asked. With the data provided by Lawrence, we can study a civilization that lived on a planet that once existed between Mars and Jupiter. It is now known as the asteroid belt—large and small masses of rock,

Annihilation of a Planet II

blasted apart from a land mass that was once a planet. Before their planet was destroyed, scientists had built a lab in a small area on Mars. This was billions of years ago, long before our own existence here on our planet. We call that lab the alien camp. They left records of scientific advancement we can adapt to launch us further into our understanding of the universe. These aliens on Mars left behind an alphabet and numerical symbols, which we need to decipher. It is imperative that we capture all the data and learn from it."

Another board member stood. His red hair was not much redder than his face, revealing his embarrassment over questioning the great Paul Linsdale. "Professor, sir, er ... can't you just pull the data from Lawrence from here?"

"That is also a good question," Linsdale said, "and the short answer is no." There was a slight ripple of laughter, further embarrassing the young Irishman who had asked the question. "The data are stored away in Lawrence's memory gland. We have to have Lawrence to access the data. The longer he is on that death pole, the more likely it is the data will be lost as he decays. The Cybernauts destroyed the alien lab while they were still on Mars, so we can never go there and use their technology. But Lawrence walked among the ruins. He has it all stored in his memory gland. We can learn from their mistakes as well as from their progress."

People on screen began to talk among themselves, although they could not be heard in the board room. Board members were not surprised because they had been alerted by the written proposal each of them had in hand. Goodwill strode to the podium and pounded his gavel. "Please, everyone! We can't hear you, but you need to listen carefully. Even silently, your inattention is quite rude. You should not interrupt Dr. Linsdale."

"It's all right, Martin. If someone on one of the screens has something to say, it is better to let it be said now."

A perplexed-looking man with snowy hair stood in the room that held the U.S. House Committee on Science.

Goodwill pressed a button. "We can hear you, sir."

"How can this be? I've never heard of such."

"Nor have I," a woman beside him exclaimed. "This is too much to grasp. No one on my team has ever heard about an alien camp on Mars."

"The little information we've been able to get tells us the planet blew up in an immense nuclear war," Paul said, "causing a perfect storm of sequences that combined with strong sunlight at just the right time. The sun's rays were like a burning match thrown toward fumes coming from a can of gasoline, igniting the planet. The explosion was tremendous, hurling some of the masses into our solar system, creating the large craters on the moon, wiping out the dinosaurs that once roamed freely on our planet and bringing the first ice age."

Annihilation of a Planet II

Paul could see harrumphs on the screen; the sound had been turned off again. Board members remained silent. Sensing skepticism, Paul added, "Surely we can all agree that our super underground bunkers will do no good on an annihilated planet!" One man set down his water glass, choking and coughing upon hearing the strong words.

"Their nuclear missiles were 100 times more deadly than ours, and we as humans don't need to take the same route to extinction. Earth does not need to become an asteroid belt due to our mismanagement and bad decisions."

Paul paused, and the room fell silent. The tension was palpable as he gathered his courage to give them the bottom line. "I'm asking that we send a rescue mission back to the red planet to retrieve Lawrence for our working knowledge. I'm asking for $5.5 billion for this must-have, critical mission."

Members of the board began to compare notes. Paul saw all the head-shaking, and he stalked out to the lobby. He breathed deeply. He had done his best. He went into the men's room and splashed cold water on his face. All he could do was wait. Stevens got his money without so much as one objection. All Earth, all the time. Why did people have to be so short-sighted? Learning from the past could make all the difference for the future. He walked back out to the lobby and sat on one of the sofas. Pulling out a Vitamin E cigarette, he thought briefly of the 21st century when cigarettes still contained tobacco, a substance that had been outlawed now for a hundred years. Cigarette companies had had to scramble to save their cash cows, and marijuana cigarettes had not filled the gap as people around the world became more health conscious. Non-THC hemp oil was used widely for medical purposes, and as the medical properties of MJ cigarettes became less in demand, the companies came up with another product: smokeless vitamin cigarettes.

"I don't know how we can fund an operation of that magnitude right now. We're still paying back all these joint countries for their investment failures on the last expedition, which was a big blunder," one man said.

As the discussion raged, Ortiz walked out to meet Paul. "Bum a cigarette off you, Paul?"

"Sure!" Paul pulled out a pack and Ortiz slid one out. He tapped it twice to ignite it. Taking a long pull, he exhaled it in a stream of water vapor that rose in the air, making a large vapor ring that drifted slowly away into the air and vanished. "You're wasting all your vitamins, Ortiz. You have to inhale it to get the vital nutrients."

Ortiz laughed. "I know. I just enjoy playing with the water vapor." He put his hand on Paul's shoulder. "I came out here to tell you I was able to get your Ming dynasty vase sold for $1.2 million. That shaves a small portion of the funds you need."

"That's great news, my friend!"

They high-fived in excitement, ignoring the two androids patrolling the lobby. The security guards

Annihilation of a Planet II

stopped in confusion, observing the strange custom they had seen many times in the past. After a moment they nodded to each other and went on their way. The customs of humans made no sense.

Ortiz and Linsdale finished their cigarettes, pressed them out and put them into a waste receptacle at the end of the sofa. They walked back to the board meeting as the debate raged on.

"In this case it is about the earth's sovereignty. We must always place Earth first, and second to no other planet," one young African man said, his ebony face glistening. Heads nodded in agreement as he added, "to keep Earth rich, with its natural forests, oceans and mountains."

A middle-aged woman from France continued the argument. "Man almost killed the planet with global warming, not realizing for the longest time the reality of the situation—all due to political fervor. Each of the two big political parties in the United States in the 21st century had separate teams of scientists. There were some who flatly denied climate change was happening, but there were some Republicans who said climate change was merely a cycle the earth goes through every few hundred years. The Democrats said climate change was a direct result of man's interference and bad decisions about protecting and conserving natural resources."

A white-haired, goateed man stood, one hand on the back of the chair in front of him, the other on his cane. Everyone in the room recognized the renowned astrophysicist. He spoke with a strong, sophisticated voice filtered through a Georgia drawl. "Let me not be ambiguous but transparently clear. The delicate earth balance was badly upset in those days."

He drew a vitamin D pipe from his pocket and took a long pull before continuing. "Earthquakes were up 84%. On its own, the earth can maintain its regular cycles of climate change due to volcano eruptions and earthquakes as it spins on its axis at 1,037 miles per hour, but it could not take the extra stress man created from excessive use of carbon fuel. When man is a factor in creating the change, man must be a factor in correcting it."

He shifted his weight a little and said, "I hope you don't mind an old man's taking the floor too long."

"Of course not, Dr. Moore," Martin Goodwill said. "We are honored to hear you speak."

Moore nodded his thanks. "Thank God a team of scientists finally broke through the partisan nonsense before it was too late. By the time it happened, the old saying, 'April showers bring in May flowers,' had changed to, 'April snow affects more than we know.' That's what it was like in New England and all over Western Europe. How many more hints did they need from Earth? If the earth could have talked, she would have shown she was one angry planet! She'd have put every one of our ancestors in a dirt bed six feet into her ground." He paused as laughter rolled around the table, and the people on the screens could be seen laughing, as well.

"And that folks, was the threat in centuries past. Now we face a new threat—a hidden threat—one we need to learn about. The information we need is in the data banks of Lawrence. We must retrieve him in order to learn from an ancient civilization, one that was far advanced but not smart enough to avoid annihilation by its own hands. We must retrieve Lawrence so we can learn from a civilization that once was a thriving, technical marvel. We must learn what happened so we can save ourselves."

Ortiz and Linsdale looked at each other in amazement. Neither of them expected support from such a hallowed figure as Dr. Herman Moore, widely respected by every scientist in the world.

An objection arose from a dark-haired man with flashing eyes. "But the cost—"

"The cost has just gone down," Ortiz said, interrupting the Spaniard who had begun a dissent. "Dr. Linsdale has offered from his personal collection a Ming dynasty vase to be sold for $1.2 million. I already have a buyer. That leaves a balance of—"

"Still more than $5 billion," muttered the Spaniard, interrupting.

"The fact that Dr. Linsdale is willing to put his own money into this should count for something," a Chinese woman said in soft, melodic voice.

After a few whispers among themselves, the board members agreed to fund the project. Through these entire proceedings, scientists and engineers, senators and congresspersons, cabinet members and the President of the United States remained at the edge of their seats, knowing the decision would be momentous. The proceedings had been riveting. The silent applause shown on the screens surrounding the room seemed surreal to Paul when the decision was announced. He shook hands with every member of the board after first shaking hands with Herman Moore, thanking him repeatedly for his defense of the project.

"Dear boy, I did it for the earth, not for you." Moore patted Linsdale on the shoulder. Both men turned and smiled, looking at the camera set up for a group shot of the monumental event.

3
Red Carpet

The ensuing months were filled with preparations to leave. A team had to be trained, and androids had to be carefully selected. The vehicle carrying them into space had to be retrofitted and checked, double checked and then checked again. Finally came the official, public announcement.

"This is Global News Network, GNN. I'm Charles Doherty. We have breaking news from Washington D.C. this morning. Reporting from Washington is Zig Fletcher."

"Thank you, Charles. It's been thirty years since our last expedition to the red planet, Mars. Dr. Paul Linsdale, son of the renowned Dr. Simon Linsdale, who died from two bullets shot into his chest at his lab 25 years ago, is venturing to send a three-person team with three androids to bring back our famous Lawrence. Most of you will remember it was the humanoid android Lawrence who single-handedly saved Earth from the Cybernaut attack. That was in

2222. The Cybernauts had been sent to Mars to colonize it, but they developed their own free will and decided to rule over the humans who had created them. Lawrence, learning about the plot, placed the Omega bomb in their spaceship before they took off into another solar system, blowing the craft into a supernova, leaving no trace of their existence. The Cybernauts had found out Lawrence was against them and tied him to a death pole, where he would stay until his parts decayed. Obviously, it did not occur to them that Lawrence had smuggled the bomb onto their spacecraft before they charged him with treason.

A picture of the Cybernaut spacecraft taking off from Earth showed on the screen as the reporter continued. "We do not know all the details of the current mission, but we do know the expedition team will bring Lawrence back to the new Smithsonian Museum, which will be opening soon in Boston. We're told Lawrence will work as a greeter at the front doors."

The screen split to show the reporter on one side and on the other side, Lawrence, tied to the death pole on Mars. Lawrence's eyes were closed, and his uniform was in tatters. Red soil, swept along by the wind, covered his artificial skin. "As you can see, some parts will have to be refurbished before he can take a place of honor at the new Smithsonian," Fletcher said. "Until today, scholars have debated Lawrence's famous saying about Darwin's theory of Evolution: 'Evolution, what a creation!' This is Zig Fletcher reporting. Back to you, Charles."

Annihilation of a Planet II

The news anchor smiled. "Folks, in a few short weeks the expedition will take off from Cape Canaveral in Florida for this momentous undertaking."

Moving from camera one to face camera two, Doherty changed the subject. "Also in today's news, home security has come up with a virtual electric eel that can pack a wallop of an electric shock to home invaders." On the screen came a video of two eels swirling around in midair, sometimes swimming around one another, as an actor portraying an intruder walked into a family room where children were playing. The eels went on attack, shocking the invader, who passed out on the floor from the electric charge. The children ran over to the phone, and the oldest called 9-1-1.

"Can you send the police to pick up an invader?" he said. "Our security eel knocked him out, and he's on the floor."

The voice of the dispatcher was heard on the video. "Someone will be there in five minutes. I have your address from your phone."

The children went back to playing their game and watching an old movie, *Zombies of the Stratosphere*, starring Leonard Nimoy.

The camera went back to the anchor desk, this time showing Angela Barry sitting next to Charles Doherty. "Wow!" she said, brushing her red hair back over her shoulder. "That would be great to have for those unwanted boyfriends who will not take no for an answer!"

Charles swallowed hard and looked straight into the camera. "Thanks for joining us for today's top stories. Good day."

Off the set, Angela said, "I am definitely getting that home security system." Charles looked at her grimly, then pivoted on his heel and stalked away. She crossed her arms and nodded her head quickly. *Good*, she thought. *Maybe he got the message.*

Paul and Eli sat together on the sofa, watching the movie *Jesus of Nazareth*, when the android butler came in. The couple did not notice him, so engrossed were they in the film.

Eli asked, "When do you think the second coming of Christ will be?"

"According to the Bible from the Dead Sea scrolls, not even our Lord, the Son of God, knows when the end of time will be near. Only God himself knows, and he will send his son like a thief in the night to reclaim the earth," Paul said, taking her hand and kissing it.

"Please don't think I'm being silly, but that reminds me of that old Disney picture we saw, *The Lion King*. Simba came back to take what was rightfully his kingdom from his uncle Scar. Simba brought the animal kingdom back to life from the destruction his uncle had caused to all the natural resources."

Annihilation of a Planet II

Paul put an arm around his wife's waist. "Why would I ever call you silly? That's a wonderful analogy. In fact—"

"Sorry sir!" The android interrupted. "Please, I am asking a second time for your attention.

Eli sat up straight and giggled. "Honey, please put the picture on pause." The life-sized images of Roman soldiers talking to Christ shrank and disappeared, leaving a black, 12-foot by 12-foot surface. Paul and Eli looked up at the butler in his vest and bow tie, his sleek hair combed straight back.

"What is the meaning of this interruption?" Paul asked.

"I have an urgent e-mail from the Hollywood producers at Paramount Pictures."

"What?" Eli and Paul asked together. They looked at each other with matching raised eyebrows.

"They are inviting you both to the 323rd Oscar Awards," the butler continued. "The movie industry wishes to honor you both as guests for the well-publicized mission back to Mars to retrieve Lawrence, the humanoid android that saved the world thirty years ago."

Eli jumped up and clapped her hands. "Paul! Can you imagine me on the red carpet? Aren't you excited?"

He laughed and put his arms around his wife. "Your excitement is my excitement, darling. And yes, I can imagine you on the red carpet." He swung her around.

The butler stood stiffly. "Excuse me! Sorry to interrupt, Dr. Linsdale, but how should I respond? Will you attend?"

Eli and Paul laughed again as he responded, "Yes. Inform Paramount that we will attend." They sat back down on the couch.

"Very good sir." The butler typed on his left arm with his right hand, "Invitation accepted." Pressing send, he announced, "Done," and went back to his usual duties.

"You'll have to write a speech, Paul," his wife said.

"A speech? No one said anything about a speech."

"But just in case. You never know."

"Yeah, yeah. I guess that goes with the territory at the Oscars. I'll be like those other also-rans who have a speech in their pockets just in case."

"Good." She smiled.

"After the movie," he said. He leaned back as Eli pressed a button. The screen seemed to spring to life with mirror technology that worked as a prism to generate a 3-D effect, carrying them back immediately to the time of Christ. Even the scent of the salt air washed over them as a breeze off the Sea of Galilee blew over them. Eli's hair floated around her face in the realistic breeze.

"I am Jesus of Nazareth," came a voice over the state-of-the art, surround-sound speakers. "You will heal in the name of God." As Jesus raised his open

Annihilation of a Planet II

hand, the sun rays cast between his fingers moved toward each person depicted on the screen having leprosy. All began to transform from sickly individuals with large tumors, pieces of skin falling off, scar tissue marring their features to clean, fresh skin without blemish. They no longer had the disease that had driven them into exile. They began to sob and cry.

"I am whole again!" one man shouted. He fell to his knees in front of Jesus, kissing his feet. As the man looked up at Jesus, his hair and beard seemed to gleam like gold in the sunlight. "I am whole again," the man repeated. "I can go back into town to live with my family. I haven't seen them in more than 10 years."

The others likewise dropped to their knees, thanking Jesus for this miracle of healing.

"Go now to your family and bear witness for this miracle from God," Jesus said in a strong voice that seemed to echo against the hills. "In God, nothing is impossible."

There were tears in Paul and Eli's eyes as they watched the touching scene. They felt as though they were part of the throng who watched the miracle in the film.

On the day before the 323rd Academy Awards ceremony, a reporter was welcoming viewers on television to the scene at the red carpet. At that moment, Paul and Eli Linsdale were about to be dropped off at the airport by the Orient Express space shuttle, which could arrive at any part of the world in thirty minutes.

This shuttle was the culmination of an idea expressed by President Ronald Reagan in the 20th century. It was an idea that was discarded and then resurrected near the end of the 21st century. Space shuttles holding as many as a hundred people could take off from anywhere, their intermediate destination a platform in the high atmosphere. From there they would descend back to Earth onto their ultimate destination.

Those who had taken advantage of the short period of weightlessness were asked to sit down and adjust their seat belts. Eli and Paul had time to sneak in a quick kiss without any gravitational pull before obediently sitting and buckling up.

"What a great flight," Paul said as he and Eli walked out into the airport's busy lobby. People from all over the world were walking around, looking up at the arrival and departure boards, stopping to get something to eat and looking for magazines to read on the shuttles. There was a TV on at one waiting area, and Eli noticed the announcer talking about the red carpet.

"Oh my goodness, Paul. It's already started! Are we a day late?"

"Relax, honey. That's a pre-show event. The Oscars are tomorrow. You know they like to string this out as long as they can. The stars are still trying to decide what to wear. Let's grab some coffee and something to eat while we wait for our luggage."

Annihilation of a Planet II

Paul's cell phone rang, and he put his watch to his ear. "Yes, hello."

"It's your luggage calling."

"Yes, I know. You're waiting for me at the luggage terminal to pick you up, but stand by. The missus and I decided to eat something first."

Eli put coffee in front of Paul with a smile.

"Luggage wants us to pick it up now," Paul groused. "Sometimes I think the machines are running us instead of the other way around." He spoke into the wrist watch/cell phone. "Give us ten minutes and we'll be there. Okay?" He sipped the coffee and thanked Eli.

"If you must know," the luggage said, "I did not make it to the luggage terminal. The handlers failed to remove me from the shuttle's luggage bay compartment."

"What?" Paul jumped up, spilling his coffee.

"I'm still in the Phoenix luggage bay," the luggage responded. "You must hurry to inform them. They will be departing in five minutes, and you won't have a tuxedo to wear for tomorrow night's Oscar awards."

"I'll be right back!" Paul yelled as he took off across the lobby, bumping into people as he ran. "Sorry! Excuse me! Beg your pardon." It was a litany of *mea culpas* as he made his way to the Phoenix desk. "Please stop that flight!" He pointed to the shuttle that carried his luggage. My bag was not taken off, and I need it here."

Airlines had long ago decided it was better to listen to customers in a situation such as this. In the long run it was cheaper and certainly less hassle to turn off the engines and get the forgotten item than send it ahead and incur the wrath of the disgruntled passenger. Paul's rapidly beating heart slowed a little as he looked out the big windows and saw his luggage being taken off the Phoenix. He was still out of breath from his run as he said, gasping, "Thank you so much for your courtesy."

"My pleasure, sir," the desk clerk replied.

Paul tuned his cell phone into the luggage bandwidth and heard, "Easy! Handle me with care!" He laughed at the thought of the luggage telling the handlers what to do. Yes, machines were telling people what to do, all right. He spoke into his phone. "I see you're now coming. If it's not too much to ask, in the future can you let me know sooner that you're still in the luggage chamber in the plane?"

"Oh, now it's my fault?" raged the luggage in a saucy tone.

Paul clinched his fist and pretended to bite it. He hung up on his luggage. *Can I ever get a break?* he wondered. *If I'm not arguing with my vehicle, it's with my luggage.* He retraced the route he'd run along, this time walking and muttering to himself. "I had to cancel an appointment with my primary doctor because my sealander had an appointment the same day—time for its routine inspection, an appointment it made without consulting me. It had the nerve—to use the term loosely—to tell me it was not going to cancel its appointment again, for the third time in a row, because of me. It told me to get a cab!"

He was gesturing as he talked to himself, and heads were turning as he walked. He was still mumbling when he got back to the table where Eli waited.

"Honey, you're the very picture of the absent-minded professor. What on earth is wrong?"

"Nothing's wrong now." He sat down with a sigh.

"Are you sure everything's all right?"

"Sweetheart, I'm so glad we never argue or fight." He leaned across the table and kissed her.

"Wow! What was that for?"

He just smiled and said, "Let's go check into our hotel and get ready for the Oscars. I've ordered our luggage to be placed in a sealander waiting for us at the curb."

As they walked down the arrival gate, they saw a handler putting their luggage into the trunk of a Nissan sealander.

"Where to?" the sealander asked.

"Pacific Sea Hollywood Crown Plaza Hotel," Paul said.

This was one of several skyscrapers that floated on the ocean like a bottle floating upright in the water. Solar panels at the top of each building delivered all the energy needed to run the water and lights for businesses and clients staying there. At the base of each building was a computer that allowed streams of jet propulsion water to keep it at a stable anchor position without it ever floating away, even under the influence of high moon tides or waves—like a finger keeping the balance of a basketball always steady, from its spin.

Paul thought about the wonders of the ocean hotels. "You know, Eli, back in the twenty-first century, the lack of water in California was a huge problem."

"Yes, dear."

"No, really. Away from the state beaches, where tourists and locals gathered to enjoy the sun and sand, water ports were built. In 2011 California had been losing 12 million acre feet of water a year. They could no longer rely on snow and rain from the atmospheric river that made landfall for fresh water. The water ports pumped ocean water into desalination plants. Then the water was distributed across the state by pipelines or trains that could haul 210 water tanks to manmade reservoirs. California had to learn from Israel and other mid-eastern countries, taking the motto, 'We must take the desert or the desert will take the state.' In 2016 San Diego embarked on a billion-dollar project that provided 50 million gallons of drinking water a day for San Diego County. They were a model for other desert counties and states that had access to ocean water."

Eli smiled and kissed her husband. "I love you, sweetheart, but you are such a wonk." She ordered the sealander to put on some country pop music. Paul smiled. His wife was a country girl at heart. As they approached the Crown Hotel, Paul considered its magnificent proportions; it was a floating city, having nearly two million people living and working there. The sealander dove beneath that water and entered through a lock and the undersea entry through a spiral door, which opened as they entered and quickly closed behind them. The water that came in with the sealander was pumped out, drying the chamber before it elevated them to the floor 26 stories high.

Exiting the sealander from the rotating seat, Paul stood with his hand out for Eli. She got out, and they shared another quick kiss as the luggage was taken out of their vehicle by android handlers.

Paul's bag was mumbling, "Oh, it's all my fault."

Paul gave the luggage a backward kick, and it fell silent.

Eli looked at her husband quizzically. "Fighting with your suitcase, Paul?"

"You wouldn't understand, dear," Paul replied. He offered his arm. "Shall we?" He guided her to the check-in counter.

"How may I assist you?" the desk clerk asked.

"I have reservations for two."

"Name?"

"I'm Paul Linsdale, and this is my wife, Eliven."

"Yes, we've been expecting you, Dr. Linsdale." Smiling, the clerk handed Paul the microchip key. "Your room number is 4A, facing the Pacific Ocean, north end. Enjoy your stay."

"May I have a key also?" Eli asked.

"Of course, ma'am." The clerk gave her a microchip key.

"Are you expecting to go somewhere without me?" Paul asked.

"No, but if you get tied up with business discussions, I may want to come back to the room without you. I know you, Paul. If you get embroiled in some kind of discussion about your Mars trip, you'll be there all night."

Paul laughed and put his arm around her waist. "You know me well, my darling."

The clerk smiled, too. "We have a complimentary dinner for you as special guests, to be served on the balcony tonight. From your room there is a spectacular view of the moon as its rays touch the water. It cannot fail to touch the hearts of lovers."

"That sounds wonderful," Eli said.

"If heaven and earth collide tonight, so be it," Paul said, looking into her eyes. "I shall die happily in your arms, my love."

Eli's pupils dilated to hear those loving words from her husband. He was never ashamed to say such sweet words in the presence of others. She felt so lucky to have this man as her husband.

Eli spoke to the android carrying their luggage to 4A. "Bring us your best bottles of reds and whites from your wine cellar."

"Will do, miss."

Annihilation of a Planet II

They looked around their hotel suite. "Cozy," Paul said in appreciation as he brought Eli close and kissed her deeply.

She stepped back with a smile. "I'm going to freshen up. Don't go away. She headed for the bedroom, pulling her luggage behind her. Paul noticed her luggage was silent, and he briefly considered swapping bags with her.

Paul stepped into the half bathroom off the sitting room. He splashed cold water on his face and grabbed a towel for drying. Noticing two electric toothbrushes on the counter with labels stating, "Compliments of Hollywood Crown Plaza Hotel," he decided to brush his teeth. He removed the plastic seal, ran the brush under a stream of water and applied toothpaste. As he started to brush, a voice startled him. "A little more to the back molars. Now up toward the incisors—"

"No!" Paul turned off the toothbrush and held it in front of his face. "Can't I brush my teeth without your help?" he yelled.

Elli came into the sitting room and peered around the bathroom door. "What did you say, honey?"

"Oh, nothing. Just having a conversation with a toothbrush. What's the world coming to? Pretty soon we'll have talking dishes that will say, 'Oh, wait, you missed a spot,' when they're being washed." He closed his eyes, imagining himself hurling a plate across the room, breaking it into smithereens.

Eli laughed. "Maybe we could get plates that would tell us when we were piling on too much food."

"Do not tease about a thing like that," Paul said in mock seriousness. "That would surely drive me over the edge."

On the opposite side of the country, in the Atlantic Ocean, unmanned subs had reached the floor of the ocean where the stacks had been discovered. They were reminiscent of the stacks of rocks found in the arid western United States—seen in old John Wayne movies—where surging water had once been. The spirals around them showed where water had once swirled around them. These dry land stacks of rocks were no longer a danger to man, but the ones beneath the ocean were directly related to the formation of hurricanes, as Dr. George Stevens had explained to the IBCPS and the audience of scientists and engineers.

The subs trained spotlights on the stacks, targeting them to be leveled. Cold fusion laser rays fired directly at the stacks demolished them into fragments that instantly littered the ocean floor.

Stevens turned from the large, flat screen monitor as the last of the rubble settled to the bottom. "There we have it, folks, the end of the massive hurricanes, saving billions of lives and businesses, unless it is brought by God Himself, whose force is unstoppable!"

Annihilation of a Planet II

People in the room raised their glasses of fine wine in celebration of the event.

A young blond man with flashing white teeth smiled into multiple cameras, saying, "Welcome, ladies and gentlemen to the 323rd Academy Awards. Tonight stars will gather from all over the world, and we have viewers like you sitting in front of TVs all over the world."

People in the bleachers yelled and cheered. The scene hadn't changed much in more than 300 years. Cameras were ready, waiting for favorites to walk down the red carpet.

"I'm told there are two special guests her tonight," the announcer continued. "Dr. Paul Linsdale and his wife, Eliven, will join us. Mrs. Linsdale is as beautiful as any movie star, and she will soon grace the red carpet."

The crowd went wild, cheering and clapping. A parade of sealanders began to arrive, stopping to deposit their contents and moving on to allow the next vehicle to come front and center. There were many models of sealanders—Ford, Tesla, Mercedes, Nissan, Toyota and General Motors brands, each with its unique style and qualities.

As the Linsdales were escorted from their limo, the crowd cheered as loudly as it did for any Hollywood star. Paul and Eli waved in appreciation as they walked down the red carpet. Paul looked handsome in his navy blue tuxedo and pale blue, pleated silk shirt and matching cummerbund. Eli was stunning in an off-one-shoulder, figure-hugging gown of white, covered with leaded crystal beads. Lights shining off the crystals sent rainbows shimmering around her. Videos and still shots buzzed and snapped as the pair walked into the building. Three photo drones the size of hummingbirds competed for the best shot of each couple that came into the building. Female actors were in competition for being the most fashionable, but of course on camera they were nothing but complimentary to each other. Men's tuxedos were not as varied, although a few seemed to be trying to make a fashion statement of some sort. Most failed. Paul Linsdale would find himself at the top of the list of fashionable men in the following day's newspaper and online accounts of the Oscars.

Hollywood stars worked the crowd, but all seemed genuinely pleased to share the space with the Linsdales. Like most people around the world, the Hollywood crowd was appreciative of Dr. Linsdale's taking on his father's role in life, continuing man's progress as well as monitoring changes that might stop advancements in technology. Back in the 20th century, Steve Wozniak and Steve Jobs were geniuses with whom the masses fell in love. Paul Linsdale seemed to be feeling the same kind of love from the people.

Eli squeezed Paul's arm. "I feel like the queen of England, married to you."

He looked at her with a soft smile, saying, "Thank you, honey. I wouldn't be what I am without

Annihilation of a Planet II

you in my life. I'll love you till the end of our time here."

She hugged him as they approached famous actors, movie producers and directors, exchanging handshakes and smiles. The Linsdales were escorted to their table, surrounded by superstars. The night was filled with excitement. Throughout the dinner—complete with fine wine—actors, directors, writers, composers and producers were called up on stage to receive their Oscars. This was recognition from their peers for superior talent shown while portraying both the famous and the not-so-famous who lived a life of hardships and tribulation, whether rich or poor, throughout the world in every aspect of life.

As the last applause died down in celebration of the award for Best Picture, the host stepped forward again. "Tonight we are graced with the presence of Dr. Paul Linsdale, who is in charge of sending an expedition team to Mars to bring back our hero Lawrence, who is now only a shell of his former self, to be placed at the new Smithsonian Museum in Boston. Every visitor there will be able to meet this amazing humanoid android who saved our planet from destruction thirty years ago. Let's put our hands together in a warm welcome for Dr. Paul Linsdale."

Paul leaned over and kissed Eli, then stood and made his way to the stage. Everyone in the audience stood and applauded as he hurried up the steps. Paul reached center stage and waved, then shook hands with the host, who handed him a great achievement award.

"Wow! I mean wow!" Paul said, shaking his head. "Thank you all!" He held up the plaque and gestured toward Eli. "And to my beautiful wife, Eliven!" He blew her a kiss as camera lights flashed and photo drones swirled through the air like hummingbirds fighting over nectar.

"I am flattered to be here to see all the stars, and being last on the program, I'm grateful the academy finally figured out how to cut the program down to a mere three hours." Laughter rippled across the room. "I grew up watching the Oscars on our family TV, and we kept track of the upcoming stars and the ones who had made it. I am amazed to be part of this show tonight. I never dreamed it could happen to me."

He ducked his head and smiled. "I wasn't invited here tonight to talk about any of that. I think you want to know about the rescue of Lawrence." Cheers interrupted him. "The project—we're hoping without any delays—will launch on September 11th. We chose that date as a symbol for healing old wounds in United States history, when the Twin Towers went down in New York. We continue to remember those 3,000 lives taken on that tragic day. We know picking this date is no more than a Band-Aid, but it means a lot to me, personally, to link it with this mission."

There was silence in the room. "I just can't pass up this chance to share a poem I wrote long ago. I believe it captures the soul and heart of all you great actors. I would like to read it and give your golden statue a voice. I acknowledge that great movies are also remembered by great music compositions, from

Annihilation of a Planet II

the days of silent movies to now. This golden statue has been the prestige award, symbol of superior achievement recognized around the world. Its acquisition even brought a tear to the eye of one legendary icon of pop culture in the 20th century—the man known as the Duke—John Wayne. He was named Best Actor at the 1970 Oscars for his 1969 film *True Grit*." Applause interrupted. "I wrote this," Paul continued, "remembering the Duke, icon of the 20th century, but in addition, the poem honors great filmmakers, producers, composers and directors who have shared in this award. But first—" Paul held up a finger and grinned, encouraging the audience to laugh—"I'll quote the Latin phrase shown over the MGM lion's head, 'Ars gratia artis.' Well, actually, the MGM writers got in wrong, it should read 'Ars Artis gratia,'" as I'm sure all you Latin scholars know." Again the audience laughed. "Either way, the translation is 'Art for art's sake.' Now for the poem." Paul took a deep breath. "I call this poem 'Life of an Actor.'

Actors will put aside their own true character
to slip in and out of other characters
that they portray for our entertainment,
amusement and pleasure.
To help educate us away from
past tyrants and future tyrants
and help us closer toward
good-willed men and women.
For these great actors will
bring into our lives
moments in time and history,

which we can only perceive.
For the world is
too large and grand
to learn all that there is.
The actor of a true character
will manifest himself or herself
into the lives of those that are
living or have passed away.
Walking in their footsteps
in sadness or happiness
an actor rises like
the northern lights.
Like a comet trailing
high above the starlight.
We acknowledge the
actors of true character
for their skill,
love and beauty
for the lives that they have portrayed.
Let us then put our hands together
and clap the actor of true character
into the Hall of Fame.
Where their names will transcend
on the lion's roaring mane!

Paul tapped his watch, and the Metro Goldwyn Mayer lion, Leo, appeared near him, roaring. The crowd was silent for a brief moment, before exploding in a cacophony of shouts and applause. They stood, still cheering and clapping. Paul tapped his watch again, and the virtual lion disappeared.

The host strode out on stage and shouted over the crowd, "It doesn't get any better than that! Poetry like that is what we mere mortals only dream of experiencing!" He shook Paul's hand, and as Paul made his way back to Eli, the host said, "We'd like to thank the billions of people watching on television and all our distinguished guests here tonight. We'll see you right back here next year! Let me remind you that the Hollywood industry is one in which humans will always be important. There will always be jobs in acting or behind-the-scene movie production. Robots lack emotions. They cannot act on instinct. Even an untalented actor can out-act an android!"

People were filing out as the last words were delivered. Some rolled their eyes at the comment, wondering if he, perhaps, had anyone in particular in mind when he referred to untalented actors.

4

Protests and Speculation

"Welcome to Global News Network's Top of the News," Charles Doherty said, as the camera zoomed in to his face. I'm Charles Doherty …"

"… and I'm Angela Barry. We're reporting tonight from GNN headquarters in New York." Angela smiled at the camera, then replaced the smile with a serious look. "The World Wildlife Fund is fighting to preserve the Amazon rainforest, the Asian rainforest, the Indonesian rainforest and Canada's Black Bear rainforest. Known as the four largest rainforests in the world, they hold unknown plant remedies—cures and treatments for illnesses and conditions of all kinds."

As Angela spoke, scenes from the rainforests showed on the screen.

"We learned today that the World Wildlife Fund is combining efforts with the Food and Drug Administration, creating a powerful team of men and

Annihilation of a Planet II

women who vow to stop the bleeding of the earth of its natural resources. The two organizations are coming together to protect the earth, thus making future needed drugs available as well as protecting wild life and indigenous people."

"That's a big undertaking, Angela," Charles said. "How are they going to accomplish all that? Those are big areas of land."

"That's right, Charles, the four rainforests do cover a wide area. I'm given to understand a lot will rest on the willingness of the indigenous people to sound the alarm. This is framed as a way for them to maintain their traditional way of life."

Scenes of the natives going about their daily lives came on the screen as Angela continued to speak. "For the past 250 years, palm oil has been the most widely produced vegetable oil worldwide. The reason: it has a high yield and is the cheapest vegetable oil to produce. But there's a hitch—oil palms need a rainforest climate and a lot of land to thrive. For this reason, palm oil plantations for that entire length of time have been the leading cause of rainforest destruction. As long ago as 2030, the natural rainforests in Malaysia and Indonesia, ceased to exist."

A scene of a family of orangutans playing together came on the screen, and Angela seemed to choke as she went on." These creatures, the orangutans, have become virtually extinct in the wild. Hundreds of them were buried alive, and elephants were burned in massive clear cuts. The orangutans that survived were considered pests, and they were clubbed to death by palm plantation workers. Only in some last bastions of rainforests in Brazil can they still be found, but rarely. Elephants and tigers that once lived in rainforests have nearly been wiped out as well. We knew this would happen! The World Wildlife Fund warned of this all the way back in 2015!"

The camera moved back to show Angela's face, showing her look of determination as she proceeded. "Now with this new program of vigilance, when men and bulldozers cross the lines to fell timber, the people who live there will report them. This aspect of the effort has already gone into effect, although at this point it is only practice. Incredibly enough, the new laws will not go into effect for three months. Congresses and parliaments insisted that businesses needed that much time to finish projects they have already started."

Bulldozers were seen pushing trees across deforested land.

"Contractors are working feverishly around the clock," Angela continued, emotion making her voice husky. "Man's greed, coupled with his hunger for palm oil, is the cause of this frenzy of activity. Palm oil is used in nearly every product we use these days. I even found it this morning on the label of my so-called *natural* peanut butter! We are literally committing suicide by tearing down natural resources that could bring cures for terrible illnesses. When are we going to learn? This is just ignorance!"

Annihilation of a Planet II

The camera panned back to Angela, showing a tear in her eye and passion written on her face. Charles was giving her a startled look.

"Um. Sorry," she said. "I guess I got a little carried away. Charles?"

"Yes. Well," Charles replied, stunned into a brief pause, "in other news today, humans are being retrained to build vast city structures due to the high cost of repairing mechanical humanoids. Parts are expensive to replace. Humans may get fractures or wounds, but the body can eventually repair itself with the proper treatment. These expensive humanoids are better suited for home comfort needs. They are easily damaged by moisture and high magnetism, which disrupt their computer chips, keeping them from working correctly. The U.S. Congress is set to pass the bill shortly, making this the law of the land. Under the new law, androids will be kept indoors in protective buildings, used only as they were originally intended, for indoor work, executing household chores. Let's join Zig Fletcher on the Mall in Washington."

"Charles, this will be the sixth try at passing this bill," Fletcher said. "We have here today a demonstration of the speed at which congress acts."

The camera panned to a tortoise slowly making its way toward a bowl of salad.

"People have been standing around all day, making friendly bets on whether congress will act before Sammy the Turtle gets to the salad," Zig explained.

"Poor thing!" Angela broke in. "Has he been walking down the Mall all day without anything to eat or drink?"

Zig laughed. "Good question, Angela. People have set small dishes of water in front of him from time to time, but he seems pretty set on getting to that salad."

The camera stayed on Sammy, who had reached the salad and was staring into the camera as he ate a leaf of lettuce. Zig Fletcher's face came back to the screen.

"All signs point to the bill's passing this time around. Humanoid androids will no longer be used in outdoor work. There are several aspects to the repercussions of this bill," Fletcher said. "First, many families are in dire straits because construction jobs have been taken away. Ordinary, hard-working citizens have found themselves living in someone's attic—those are the lucky ones—or living in their cars. They lost their homes shortly after losing their jobs. Their families are under a great deal of stress."

A scene was shown of a family sitting in a car, surrounded by their belongings and detritus of a meal.

"Second," Fletcher continued, "the robots have proved to be dangerous in many respects. Old fashioned police guns and rifles are now used against wayward androids. The bullets have to be retrofitted with a seal of magnets coating the shells and a few droplets of water inside. When fired at an android

Annihilation of a Planet II

gone amok, such a bullet will puncture a robot's metallic body, damaging its circuit board.

A clip of police officers bringing down a 10-foot robot came to the screen.

"This android went haywire after it got caught in a heavy downpour of rain, disrupting its mechanical brain. There were two casualties among the police officers. The remaining seven officers unloaded their retrofitted .45 magnums, which have been resurrected after a 150-year hiatus. It now has a new type of bullet made especially for use against the machines."

On the screen the giant construction robot fell to the ground, sparks bursting from its chest and shoulders.

"Even with a body of waterproof material built into the armor," Zig's voice said over the continuing scene of the police and the robot, with two officers being taken to hospitals, "sometimes moisture will get into the android, damaging these expensive machines. That's what happened here."

The camera came back to Fletcher. "Only the late Dr. Simon Linsdale was able to design his late prototype of androids, known as Cybernauts, with a protective Kevlar coating of anti-moisture and anti-magnetic material, but his secret formula was lost with him in his lab long ago. And that's why, we speculate, his son wants to bring back Lawrence—to analyze his artificial skin. Then and only then will we have androids back working at construction sites. We suspect Lawrence has the top secret formula."

Still on camera, Zig walked over to a short, husky man with dark curly hair and dark eyes. "I am here now, live, with Vincent Marini, a construction superintendent for a building project on the Mall.

"I'm against letting the robots take away our jobs again," Marini said. "Once this law has passed, won't there have to be another Act of Congress to let them back on work sites?"

Another man walked up and clapped Marini on the shoulder. He leaned over into the microphone. "If an Act of Congress is necessary, we'll have our jobs for a long time." He laughed and moved away.

Zig laughed, too, but Vincent Marini did not laugh. "We must stop Linsdale," said the union worker, "or they will take away from us what we are just now getting back—a growing human economy. If new robots are redesigned with the protective skin, they'll take our jobs!"

Watching from a beer hall down the street, an old man with a gray beard and pony tail slammed down his beer. "He's right!" the man declared. "We must take action. Who's with me?"

Three other men approached him, and they began to talk about what to do next. A group formed, and they set out toward Linsdale's lab. This route took them along the specially made sidewalks that went over the Tesla belt roads where sealanders below were traveling in different lanes, ranging in speed from 10 to 100 miles per hour. Where there were once dirt lanes, gravel roads and tarmac roadways on

Annihilation of a Planet II

a single plane, now the Tesla belts wove over and around each other like strands of spaghetti.

Fuel for the Tesla system was paid as a household utility invoice each month, added to the household electric bill as a surcharge per mile driven, automatically sent to the electric company. The companies worked under old, familiar names—Shell, Mobil and Chevron. The sealanders could go 200 miles off-road without needing recharge, such as when they had to dive underwater to their destination.

The group of protestors marched up to the front of Linsdale's science lab, where security forces kept them back with virtual screens operated by particles of light. Some protestors held signs that read, "Keep indoor jobs for 'bots." Others read, "Leave hard jobs to real men and women."

Paul walked out to the crowd that had gathered in front of his lab. To keep his late father's legacy strong, he had kept the name C and L Automation (for Computerized & Laboratory Automation). "May I please have your attention?" He loosened his tie. "Trust me. We are not going to Mars to get Lawrence to study the man-made skin fiber my father formulated. Lawrence's skin has disintegrated," Linsdale said, exaggerating the extent of decay of Lawrence's outer layer. "All he has remaining is his mechanical frame. I do not plan to remake the special skin the other 900 robots had. Your jobs are safe and will forever remain safe."

One person wearing a construction hat yelled, "Why should we believe you?"

"You will have to take my word on that, sir!"

"That's not good enough!" the man yelled back.

As the crowd started shoving forward, the police riot squad stood shoulder to shoulder, shields up, pushing back. Paul headed back with his team of scientists—about a dozen—following him into the building. He spoke to his team. "Now that the media are well involved in our mission, we need to stay silent on everything we do. Is that clear?"

"Yes," nearly everyone said. One young woman nodded her head slightly.

Dr. Linsdale looked at her and directed the question to her. "Is that understood, Dr. Iceland?"

The petite, dark-haired woman quickly put a hand in the pocket of her lab coat and pulled out a neck band that carried sensitive microchips. These chips picked up vibrations from her inner voice. She clipped on the band with both hands, positioned the tiny crystals over her voice box area and replied in a sweet voice, "Yes, Dr. Paul. I hear you loud and clear. My hearing aid is working. I forgot to put my vibe-vascular neck brace back on after cleaning it. I will be getting a permanent one soon. The surgery is next month, in fact. And I won't need to wear these necklaces …" She looked around and winked. Well … maybe just for fashion's sake." As she began to laugh, everyone joined her.

An hour later Paul and his team gathered around a television set in the lab to see how the scene would play on the news.

Annihilation of a Planet II

"I hope we're on first," a tall man wearing horn-rimmed glasses said. My wife is freaking out because someone told her there was a riot here today, and I'm going to stop by to pick up some flowers for her on the way home."

"Have you programmed your sealander, Jimmy?" Elizabeth Iceland asked with a laugh.

"You know me well, Liz. Of course I programmed the sealander. I did it as soon as I cut the connection with my wife. I know as well as you do that I'm the original self-absorbed scientist."

The GNN logo came up on the screen, and the team fell silent.

"Welcome to Global News Network's Top of the News," Charles Doherty said, smiling into the camera. "The lab rebuilt by Dr. Paul Linsdale was under fire today as protesters demanded the dumping of the expedition team set to go to Mars to bring back Lawrence. Speculation among the demonstrators was that the mission is a cover up for sampling the specialized skin on Lawrence so it can be reproduced. The skin on Lawrence and those 900 Cybernauts he killed when they went rogue was resistant to water and magnetic interference. Conspiracy theorists say this is the only reason the International Board of Climate and Planetary Science, in partnership with the International Monetary Fund, are funding the mission. Stay tuned."

He turned to his co-anchor. "Angela, we also have breaking news on the education front. Let's—"

The flat screen TV snapped off and Linsdale shook his head in disbelief. "We're going to have to move up the date so the crowd does not know when to try their intervention. We want no mishaps on the day of the launch. It's a calculated risk, but we have to do it."

He turned to Elizabeth. "Dr. Iceland, please inform Cape Canaveral without delay. New launch date is September 8." She nodded and walked a little away from the group to speak into the phone on her wrist.

Linsdale looked around at the other scientists as their agitated body language and excited remarks to each other showed their dismay. Waving his hands in the air for silence, he said, "The world thinks the launch will be on September 11th. I know I will have a lot to answer for, but that's how we ride this event. From this point on, no interviews. These reporters will be digging for clues, and we shall give them none. Nothing. Nada. Zilch. Got it?"

Each one offered a version of agreement. "Yep!" "You bet." "Yes, sir." "Got it." Paul shook hands with each of them, including Elizabeth Iceland as she returned and nodded, affirming that the new date had been passed along to NASA. Linsdale walked into his office and sat for a moment, closing his eyes and praying he was doing the right thing.

A few minutes later he was walking out the front door, saying goodbye to the guards. His sealander

Annihilation of a Planet II

wheeled up at two miles per hour, the hatch door opening and the seat swiveling out. As soon as Paul was seated and was safely inside, his vehicle rolled over to the Tesla belt, retracted its wheels and accelerated from five to fifty mph in three seconds. Two seconds later it was on the express belt going 100 mph. Paul sat back, pushed a button for Brahms and fell asleep.

Twenty minutes later the sealander cut into the music with an alert. "Dr. Linsdale, we're nearly home, and we have company."

Paul sat up quickly and looked toward his home. A crowd of protestors were lined up around the outside of the lake with signs held aloft. A large one read, "Mars Mission Stops Here!"

"TV on!" Linsdale said, and a screen came down from the sealander's ceiling. Zig Fletcher was shown at the center of the crowd.

"This is live, breaking news from GNN," Fletcher said. "We are at the estate of Dr. Paul Linsdale, where protestors have gathered to try to stop the manned mission to Mars."

People were chanting in unison, "Mankind first! Mankind first! Mankind first!"

The camera panned around the angry crowd. "Folks," Zig said, excitement in his voice, "the esteemed professor is returning to his home right this moment." Fletcher was again on screen. "Let's see if we can get Dr. Linsdale's reaction to this protest." Fletcher began to run toward the sealander, his cameraman jogging behind him. The TV screen was given over to a camera that was tracing the reporter and his cameraman, racing to get to the lake before Linsdale's sealander.

"Submerge," Paul said, and the sealander dove into the watery tunnel beneath the lake, five yards ahead of the reporter. It shot up through the water like a porpoise and motored toward the dock, a boat on a pond that was placid except for waves made by its entrance from below. Linsdale stepped out on dry land and looked back at the crowd a mere hundred yards away. He spoke into the cell phone on his wrist, instantly activating water jets along the outside perimeter of the lake. A wall of water three stories high began to circulate from the lake and back into the lake—a fountain that would continue until the orders were given to cease. The crowd could no longer be seen or heard by anyone in front of the house.

"Ahh! That's better," Paul said. "Peace and quiet at last. It's amazing how the negative ions of rushing water can soothe the soul."

Eli was watching from a second story window. "Really?" she mouthed. Her hands were on her waist and she shook her head.

Paul looked up at her, shrugging and smiling as though to say, "What else could I do?" He ambled into the house as she hurried down the stairs to greet him with a kiss. Arm in arm they walked upstairs and out onto the deck to watch what was happening across the lake.

Annihilation of a Planet II

People were furious, and being wet made them even angrier. As they hustled to their sealanders, looking into the trunks for towels or anything else with which they might dry off, they cursed and pumped their fists into the air at the wall of water.

Eli picked up a remote and turned on the TV, set to GNN. "I'm Zig Fletcher, soaking wet"—he caught a towel someone threw to him—"and I'm signing off for now. The world renowned Dr. Paul Linsdale obviously does not want to speak to us. You can rest assured, however, that we will follow up with this story, wet or dry. Back to you, Charles."

Eli turned off the TV, and Paul offered her a Vitamin E cigarette. They relaxed on the outdoor swing, moving slightly. Eli stood. "Would you like a Scotch?" she asked.

"That would be nice."

She poured the Scotch into a glass slightly larger than a shot glass and handed it to her husband, who downed it in one quick gulp.

"Thank you, honey." He set the glass down on a table beside the swing as she sat back down. He turned to her. "I am done talking to the media, Eli. They are being disruptive to what I am trying to do. This is not a yes or no game. It is—"

"Oh, honey!" She interrupted him with a hug. "You don't have to explain yourself to me. You are right, and you are such a confident leader. I love you."

"Thanks, sweetheart," he replied. "At least you agree. When I'm wrong, you let me know. And when I'm right, you simply embrace me, as you're doing now."

5

A Change in Plans

In an old, beat up Ford sealander, the gray-bearded and pony-tailed man from the bar watched activities at Cape Canaveral with binoculars. Stationed there to report suspicious activity to his union, he and three other members had been sitting in the car together for two days; they were beginning to get on each other's nerves. They had taken turns sleeping and walking along the beach, but their own body odors were getting them down. The younger men were ready to quit; they saw no reason to keep up the vigil. But the old man insisted they were doing something important. He stared at the "No Trespassing" sign and reminded himself that the sign had always been there; it had not been put there solely for this mission to Mars.

Putting his wrist phone to his mouth, he said, "It looks as though tests are still underway for the takeoff to Mars. I see engineers doing check points on the craft."

A voice came through the speaker phone. The three other men leaned toward the wrist phone, listening carefully. "Okay. We're hoping the union lobbyists can get Congress to sign a bill to stop the mission before September 11th. They are persuading the legislators one at a time, arguing that the needs of humans are more important than the so-called efficiency of machines. And if words don't work ... money will ... we hope."

"Anything we can do to help, sir?" the old man asked.

"Just keep watching," the disembodied voice commanded.

The two men in the back of the sealander threw themselves back against the seat backs, disgusted at the thought of sitting in the car for another period of time. The man in the front passenger seat had red hair and a heavy sprinkle of red freckles across his face, giving him the name "Red," which hinted at his reputation for losing his temper. He leaned against the side window and closed his blue eyes, saying, "Wake me when you want me to take the next watch."

"No!" the old man said. "We must act now ... and fast. We can't wait on Congress. I have a hunch they will vote for the mission without delay. There's money pouring in from the other side, you know. We have to take this matter into our own hands for the security of the working people of the world."

Annihilation of a Planet II

The other three men were suddenly alert. Anything to get away from the boredom of the last few days.

"Do you feel me?" the old man asked. "Men! We'll be looked upon as heroes!"

Excitement surged through the men, rekindling the feeling that had begun in the bar the previous week. The plot was hatched with a sketchy plan to do damage to the spacecraft.

The old man gave the orders. "Each of you has a duffle bag with a pipe wrench and a black jumpsuit and mask. I also obtained an invisibility shield to throw over us as we sneak past the guards. It will work only for a few minutes, so time will be of the essence when we use it, and we have to stay close together. I'll lead you past security, and we'll go straight to the control panels and start hammering away at them. It'll take months to repair them. That will give those prissy-ant lobbyists time to pay off Congress to disapprove the launch."

"How do we get out without getting caught, boss?" one of the men in the back seat asked.

Red laughed. "We'll get caught, jackass. There's no way we go in there and hammer like fools without getting caught."

"What's the matter with you?" the old man added. "We're doing this for state and country … for mankind. We'll get a little jail time, but the union will bail us out. We'll get community service work, then we're good."

The men stepped out of the sealander to put on the jumpsuits. Pulling out the wrenches, they threw the duffle bags back into the sealander.

"Follow me," the old man said, "and be quiet. We've got a five-mile walk ahead of us."

"Five miles? Crap!" One of the men said.

"Shut up!"

Low grumbling.

At the end of the long walk, the old man signaled them to get close together for the invisibility shield. They hunched down together and walked through the entrance at the lift side; the gate was open.

Two guards stood to the right side of the gate. "Did you see the ground move over there?" one of them asked the other.

"What?"

"Over there! Just a second ago."

I hope you're not drinking on the job again, Blaine."

"Oh, come on. That was one time, after my 10-year-old's birthday party."

"Keep doing that, Blaine."

"I'm telling you, I saw something."

"Okay! Let's patrol around the grounds and meet up back here in 15 minutes."

They began to walk the circumference of the grounds, each going in a different direction.

Annihilation of a Planet II

The four intruders in black hurried to the first building and looked in. A security guard was inside playing cards with a security android.

"Oh, crap! I need to win at least one fold tonight!" the human security guard exclaimed. "Do me a favor. Put your brain setting to level one. At least then I'll have a chance. I can't keep up with you at level two yet."

"Okay. I've reprogrammed my level of thought to level one," the android said.

The human stretched. "Let's take a quick break."

The android looked confused. "Break? That does not register."

"I guess at level one you won't get a lot of stuff. I'm going to take a break and I'll be right back. I'm going to the john."

"Who's John?"

"I'm going to the restroom. I'll be right back."

As soon as the guard was out of sight, the intruders made their move. "Come on!" the old man said. "Move!" He ran in with a child's super-soaker in his hand, aiming jet propelled water at the android's exposed electrical circuits. It fought back for a moment, sending one man into the wall. Sparks began to fly from the android's neck, and suddenly its body went into a frozen state and collapsed.

The noise of the crash brought the human guard from the rest room, a club in one hand and a gun in the other. Red and the old man were hiding behind the counter where they had dragged the android. The old man crawled on all fours so he was behind the guard as he ran up to the counter. Red jumped up and pushed him backward, over the old man.

"You won't get away with this!" the guard yelled. "You're going to face some big—"

Red's fist stopped the warning, and they dragged the guard around to hide him behind the counter with the android.

Using the emergency staircase, the four men made their way up to the third floor where the circuit boards were kept. The old man had done his homework. He knew not to use the elevators. They were surely a trap. Unfortunately for him and his co-conspirators, he had not done quite enough homework. Security cameras on the staircases pinpointed their whereabouts and dispatched androids as soon as they entered the third floor. Their large pipe wrenches were stripped from their hands.

"Doggonit, Red!" the old man yelled. "Why didn't you use the water soaker gun? I handed it to you!"

"You used all the water on the android downstairs, boss. There was no time to refill it."

Paul and Eli sat on their sofa in front of the TV to catch the end of the GNN Top of the News broadcast. To their surprise there was footage of four men in black being captured by android guards at Cape Canaveral.

Annihilation of a Planet II

"... tried to delay the space mission to Mars with heavy pipe wrenches, with which they planned to deactivate control boards on the third floor. One guard was injured and an android was badly damaged. One of the intruders was injured when the android threw him against a wall before it was taken down. If the intruders had been successful, there would have been months of delay for the mission. What began as a normal space recovery mission has now become a conflicting story. Many people are now questioning whether we should forget this mission—"

Dr. Linsdale picked up the remote and clicked off the TV. "This project cannot be delayed any longer. We launch in three days." He kissed Eli and left for the lab to make final preparations.

"This is Charles Doherty at GNN. Breaking news! At 6 A.M. Eastern Standard Time today—one week earlier than announced—the shuttle launched. These pictures are courtesy of NASA. No reporters were at the scene. The shuttle, headed for Mars, has as its mission the retrieval of the android Lawrence."

The NASA pictures faded from the screen, and the GNN anchor desk was shown. Angela Barry was seated next to Charles. He turned to her. "You have a human interest story for us this morning, don't you, Angela?"

"I do, Charles. Thank you. Last week I got an anonymous call from a woman who said she once knew Lawrence when both worked as caretakers for the elderly. After hearing the news about him, she remembered having a date with him."

A clip came to the screen showing Lawrence going about his duties as a caregiver. Angela's voiceover explained, "Here is Lawrence working with one of his patients. I must warn our viewers that the story I was told is uncorroborated. Androids are forbidden to date, but it's such an interesting story, I'd like to share it."

The camera returned to Angela's face. "The woman told me she and Lawrence went to see the movie *The Prince and I*. Afterward they walked in a rose garden, and they kissed. When they saw a comet fly high in the night sky, Lawrence asked her to make a wish."

Charles asked Angela, "Did he make a wish?"

"Yes," Angela replied, "according to my source, he did."

"Did he tell her what it was?" Charles asked.

"He said his wish was to feel human emotions—and most of all to feel love," Angela said. "That's so romantic coming from an android. I think he could teach human males a thing or two." She looked fiercely at Charles. "According to the caller, Lawrence said it was an irresistible force for which men have died, for country and state and for a woman since the beginning of time. He told her about Helen of Troy and also about Mark Anthony's love for Cleopatra. Apparently he told her other great love stories, too." Angela sighed, looking dreamy-eyed.

Annihilation of a Planet II

Charles looked uncomfortable. He cleared his throat. "Did the woman also make a wish?"

Angela nodded. "She wished she could smell the fine fragrance of a red rose."

"Then she is also an android!" Charles exclaimed.

"Yes!" Angela said. "I know this is a news show, but it is seldom we get to tell something that is good and sweet."

"Well, it's illegal if it's true," Charles said, before signing off.

The camera did not show Angela's face as she glared at Charles.

Lilah watched Angela's clip and thought again of Lawrence. Her eyes began to sparkle as she thought of the shuttle that would bring him home. The artificial heart pumping fluids of plasma regulating her system started pulsing rapidly when she heard his name. She turned away from the TV and looked at the old veteran now in her care, but she felt somehow weak. The drink she was holding out to the patient slipped out of her hand.

Thinking the look she had for Lawrence was for him, the veteran said, "Wow! You never looked at me like that before!" Becoming excited, he grabbed his false teeth from a cup of cleaning solution, shook them off and put them into his mouth, quickly puckering his lips together for a kiss.

Lilah said, "I will grab a towel to wipe this spill and get you another cold drink Mr. Carter."

She brought him another cold drink and handed it to him, and Carter sipped it as he lay back on his recliner, watching the TV. Lilah began to wipe the floor where the drink had splashed. Carter started blowing kisses to her, but she didn't notice. She finished the clean up and said, "Mr. Carter, anything else?"

He got annoyed because she was not responding to him. "Aw, go retire for the night. You can't handle this old marine general anyways, h*oo*-rah!" And he dozed off to sleep.

Lilah walked to her room thinking of Lawrence. She checked her vital signs and wondered why she felt this way after hearing his name. Did he do something to her, unknown to her, for her to act in such a way? She recalled one of his poems.

Your arms in my arms,
Your lips to my lips,
What more is there to live for,
But love.

She grabbed a decorative pillow from a love seat and hugged it, looking out into the night sky at a little glimmering red star—Mars.

Dr. Paul Linsdale had called his colleagues to meet him an hour before lift off without telling them why. He arrived first and put on coffee. He had brought pastries knowing the scientists and engineers he had summoned were going to be cranky about being summoned from their warm beds this early in the morning.

"What's this all about, Paul," a man named Sanders asked. "The launch isn't for another week.

Jimmy Elliot pushed his glasses up on his nose. "I think it's going to be sooner, Sandy. We talked about that, remember?"

"Right," Elizabeth Iceland said. "I told NASA it would be on September eighth."

Paul looked down. "Umm ... well ..." he looked at his watch ... "Ladies and gentlemen 10 minutes ago Project Yu Yan, which means Bird of the Universe, was launched into space. I named it after the beautiful Ming dynasty vase I had to sell to help make the mission possible."

The men and women turned to each other in surprise. Paul had taken on more authority than he legally had.

"What's the meaning of this, Paul?" Sanders asked. "Today is the fourth."

"I apologize for the subterfuge of launching without letting you know," Linsdale said, "but secrecy was important, and you needed plausible deniability. I needed it to be only on me. You saw for yourselves there were elements trying to stop the mission in whatever way they could. Project Yu Yan is now underway, and we will be able to track minute by minute with NASA on our telecommunication satellite. We are together now, and we can track it together. We planned it together, we outfitted and trained the team together. All I did was give the go-ahead to launch."

Paul paused to see how the team would take this new development, and they seemed to acquiesce. What choice did they have? "Let's take a break and call family or others, tell them we'll be overnighting. This is not going to be a seven-month mission as it was back in the day of early exploration. It is a three-day mission—on and off. Simple."

"Yeah. What could go wrong?" Jimmy said, laughing.

Everyone left to call home. Paul texted his wife from his watch phone. His texting took a while; finally he hit send and sat back in his chair with a smile.

Eli was sitting on the open deck when her phone chirped; she pressed open. Tiny love birds flew from her phone, circling her wrist, then her head, chirping and then vanishing back into her phone. As the last bird disappeared, a scroll rolled from the phone. On the scroll, opening like a letter, was a poem, which she read aloud.

Sunshine,
the world is a beautiful place,
but when God added you in the world
He made it extra spectacular!
Love makes a person feel good inside,
it is the pure breath of life.

Annihilation of a Planet II
Everything else just simply confuses life ...
I love you, Eli!

He had added, "Don't stay up for me. I'm stuck here at the office overnight."

She, alone, had known about the launch. She understood why he was not coming home. She wondered how his colleagues were taking the news. They expected to be treated as equals. She knew that about academic types. They did not take kindly to the concept of bosses. However, she had faith that her husband could soothe any ruffled feathers. If anyone could do it, her Paul could.

She placed her hand over her heart as she re-read the poem, and then she sent back a short message.

Everyone had gathered back in the boardroom when Paul's wrist phone chirped. Absently he pressed open, and a large, colorful butterfly flew out. It fluttered around his head, circling once, twice, three times, and then planted a kiss on his lips. Finally it dived back into the watch.

Paul's face was beet red. He looked at his shoes as he said, "Let's get down to business."

People were pressing their lips together, looking everywhere but at Dr. Linsdale, trying not to laugh.

A white-haired gentleman, Dr. Leslie Spencer, did not hold back. "Boy, don't you love these new-fangled text messages with virtual imaging?"

There was no way to hold back the laughter. Paul joined in, and from that point the group had an easy-going camaraderie that had been absent at the beginning.

6
Red Planet

The shuttle made entry into the atmosphere of the red planet, retrorockets firing as it slowly descended to the surface. A whirlwind of red cloud puffed around it. Three astronauts walked down the ramp and waved out to all the viewers on Earth by looking at a camera attached to the top of the shuttle. All over the world people were fixated on their television screens.

At NASA, Houston Mission Control, all celebrated by clapping hands.

At Linsdale's lab, his staff celebrated. "Yay! All right! We did it!"

The Astronauts' voices came over the radio. Captain Harris said, "The Yu Yan has landed."

Now even higher cheers went up around the world.

Three androids drove out of the craft on a four-wheel stellar module with a back bed attached to it. The three astronauts jumped into the module. With an android at the controls, the vehicle immediately wound around the crevices and hills, red clouds of dust billowing out behind it. Attached to its back on a high pole was a camera that allowed newscasters around the world to report the mission.

As the vehicle made its way into the city, everyone could see the ghost town built and abandoned by the Cybernauts. There was neither a living soul nor an android to be seen walking about. The stellar module bounced up and down on the rough terrain as the android steered it toward the inner capital. Tall buildings on all sides created a canyon around them. Coming within sight of the death pole, the android brought the vehicle to an abrupt stop. The captain tapped his helmet, and magnifying optics zoomed in at the death pole from yards away, showing a body hoisted high. The astronauts high fived and gave thumbs up signs to the camera. Harris spoke: "Mission Control, we have a visual."

He could hear through his head phones the cheers at NASA as he extended his arm toward the pole, commanding the android to drive forward. The vehicle lurched ahead and stopped at the foot of the pole. The entire crew got out of the vehicle and looked up at Lawrence, about three stories above them.

A sudden cracking noise sounded behind them, and pieces of a tall building fell around them and over them, scattering debris in a cloud of red dust. They ran for cover ... but there was no cover. They seemed to disappear in a flurry of red rocks and dirt.

Annihilation of a Planet II

"This is Mission Control. Please report status." The request reverberated in everyone's head phones.

Harris was too busy to answer. He, himself, was trying to figure out the status. "Put on your infrared scanners so you can see," he said to his team. The androids engaged their infrared scanners, and the astronauts put theirs on. "Now let's see how everyone is. Anyone injured? Are we all here?"

"This is Mission Control. Please report status." This time the request seemed more desperate.

"This is Yu Yan. No casualties," Harris said. "All humans and androids are accounted for. We are moving back to the foot of the death pole … Here we are. Ready for taking Lawrence down." They looked up at Lawrence, his withered body seeming to decay before their eyes.

"Androids, spread out. Position yourselves 40 feet apart like points in a triangle. Engage hooks at the top of the pole, one at a time."

With pinpoint accuracy the hooks attached to cables sailed over Lawrence's head and grasped the plasitron material at the top of the pole.

"Excellent!" Harris said. "Pull tight and don't allow any slack." He looked at the other two astronauts. "Diaz and McClure, start cutting through the base with the laser cutters."

High intensity blue indigo lights shot from their radon guns as Diaz and McClure aimed at the Kevlar ion base that held the pole in place. After about five minutes the metal turned as red as fire, and slowly it began to break. After another five minutes it gave way, and the pole broke free from the base that had held it. The androids kept the pole balanced as it popped away and then onto the red ground. It rocked back and forth as the androids worked together, grasping the cables wrapped around their hands and shifting their legs back and forth, moving their knees up and down.

"Don't give way! Hold your positions!" Harris yelled.

Lawrence's body swayed back and forth in the air, away from the pole, as the androids struggled to maintain control. Finally they were able to steady it. "Good job, androids! Now Android One, walk the pole down and to the north. Two and Three, you keep it balanced and secure, with its base on the ground."

At last the pole, with Lawrence on top, was resting on the ground.

This entire scene was captured for people around the world. An elementary school classroom had a large screen TV on which the red dust seemed so real some of the children began to cough. In more than one home a child looked up at her parents and said, "Mom and Dad, I want to be an astronaut when I grow up!" And the parents replied, "Why not?"

There was something on Mars that none of those children saw. Lurking in the distance, watching and waiting like a hungry bear, it moved ever closer as

Annihilation of a Planet II

the crew of six reverently untied Lawrence. The androids carefully picked up the humanoid and placed him on the back bed of the stellar module.

"So this is the great Cybernaut Lawrence," Android One said.

The words were scarcely out of his mouth when he found himself and his companions under attack. A blinding beam of light held the six-unit crew of humans and androids in its clutches.

"I can't see! Something has blinded me!" one of them cried. All six scrambled behind a building, fleeing from the pain of macular bleaching.

"Engage sun shades!" Harris yelled.

"Whew! What is that thing?" Diaz asked. "When I said I wanted to go to Arizona, I was just kidding."

"From what I can tell right now, it's nothing more than a bright light," Harris said. "Everyone fire at the light, and if need be, disarm any other weapons this thing may have."

They fired their laser fisters at the light centers of the ... whatever it was ... that had made them temporarily blind. The type of laser they were using had a stronger impact on objects than a steady surge would have had. Rather than a smooth beam of light, the laser pulsated in quick streams—rapid punches of balls of light. They quickly disarmed what turned out to be a vehicle. The astronauts walked toward it with caution, pointing the phasers at it in case of any sudden moves. Suddenly it began to careen backward on its wheels.

"Halt!" Tim Harris commanded. "What are you? And how did you get here? Did the Cybernauts create you?"

The vehicle stopped, and in halting English it said. "No ... Spirit here since 2004. Lost contact ... with NASA 2010."

"You're the missing twin rover? The Spirit?" Anna McClure asked.

"Yes! You know me?"

"Of course we know about you." Anna replied, excitement tinging her voice. "You were one of NASA's first generation exploration vehicle machines to study the terrain on Mars. NASA lost communication with you."

"Now Spirit found! Lost signal. Stayed here."

"Why did you fire at us?" Harris asked.

Spirit seemed to struggle with a way to say everything. It had not been programmed to carry on conversations. "Saw android Cybernauts ... build city ... ruined now. Cybernauts bad. Want to ... destroy Earth. They leave ... not come back ... Spirit not know why ... I hide, get information. Bad Cybernauts not get database of Spirit."

After a brief silence, Spirit continued, "I saw you ... think you are bad, too. I think I will blind you with light ... and crush you with wheels. Now see you are from NASA ... take me home.

The entire scene was avidly watched by Paul Linsdale and his team on Earth. He rubbed his head as he looked down, thinking, nodding, trying to get

Annihilation of a Planet II

his thoughts together. He turned to his console. "Tim," he said to Harris, "this is Paul Linsdale. Do you read me?"

"Loud and clear! Roger!"

"Ask Spirit what important data he has collected for the past 240 years."

As Tim Harris asked the question, TV sets around the world lost their audio and picture as static took over, like the old black and white TV sets of the mid-20th century. A signal that said 'Stand By'—or words to that effect in appropriate languages—came up on the screens of every viewing instrument in the general population of the world.

"There's big brother interrupting the message," a man yelled as he watched a TV in a bar. He threw a beer bottle at the screen and it went right through, breaking on the wall behind the TV set.

"Now you can just get over there and mop up the mess," the bartender said. "All you did was make yourself the center of attention. You didn't clear up the picture now, did you?"

Linsdale had purposely deactivated the signals away from all public communications. Only NASA, the White House and C and L Automation got the communication clearly.

"Dr. Linsdale, I can read the data for you more easily than Spirit can tell you," Diaz said. "I am well versed in the early stage rover language, and I can access its data bank."

"Very well," Linsdale said. "That will work."

"Spirit found a lost, abandoned city here on Mars that has also deteriorated into rubble. It predates our planet, and it shows a language of art and math. The creatures who built this city were from a planet that had a great habitation of plants and trees with wildlife, oceans and lakes ... before it blew up." Diaz looked up from the data. "Amazing!"

Linsdale knew about this, but he had not informed the Yu Yan team. He felt a rush of exhilaration to have his deductions corroborated. "Is that all?"

"Oh, no sir!" Diaz said. "The records Spirit gathered show the lost planet was located between Mars and Jupiter. When it became nothing more than rocks and dust, it formed the asteroid belt. This has to have happened millions of years ago. It had five moons. Two of its moons now orbit Mars, and the other three were added to Jupiter's many moons—67 that we know of—caught by those two planets' gravitational pull."

Paul turned to his team and said wryly, "It always good to get a little astronomy lesson from an astronaut." The scientists laughed. "Diaz is a good man. The young ones always get a little carried away, but it's a good thing he was on this mission. Spirit wasn't programmed to hold a conversation. That was primitive technology back in 2004."

Linsdale turned back to his console. "Tim, do you read me? Over?"

"Roger that!"

Annihilation of a Planet II

"Thank Diaz for his service. That's all for now. Get back to the live airways. The mission is complete. Bring Spirit with you to the loading bay. Thank God it is large enough to fit him in."

"Roger that!" Harris said merrily.

Linsdale restored communication to all public airwaves, and news stations interrupted their usual shows.

"Breaking news. This is GNN," Charles Doherty, announced. "We have learned that a solar ray was the cause of the breakdown of communication a few moments ago. It threw off the communication panels, but the problem has been resolved by NASA. We take you now to live coverage of the crew heading back to their module. They are the same six—three astronauts and three androids—who left Earth one week earlier than announced, plus the humanoid android Lawrence, a hero in his own right, and the long-lost twin rover, Spirit. Quite a haul, ladies and gentlemen! Stay tuned to GNN. We'll bring you all the news you need to know! Signing off for GNN, I'm Charles Doherty."

At NASA, there was pandemonium.

"Who could they have been?"

"Maybe the ancestors of the ancient Egyptians!"

"Or the Incas!

"Or the real models for Greek mythology!"

"This is unbelievable! Think about it!"

"People! Settle down!" The director of NASA shouted. He focused on the large screen monitor, watching the Mars crew as they made their way to the stellar module. "Remember, all of you, what you have heard and seen is top secret." He thought to himself, *every year at least a hundred scientists disappear, reason unknown. I don't want that to happen to people on this team, just because they can't keep their mouths shut.*

On the screen the crew on Mars seemed to be struggling to get to the shuttle. Lawrence was tied down on the back bed of the module, and Spirit was tugged along behind at the end of a cable. One of the androids was riding Spirit. This configuration made the going slower, and high winds were proving to make forward motion difficult. Astronauts and androids were being tossed around. Small whirlwinds of red dust blew against them, knocking them down. It was as though some unknown force had been sent to stop their progress.

"Get out of the module and stay out!" Harris shouted. "We have to stay close, though. Walk close together. Cut the cables on Lawrence. Androids One and Two! You carry him. The vehicle and the back bed aren't safe. These winds can get under them and just raise them up."

The android on Spirit was just getting off the old vehicle to get his orders when a powerful burst of wind picked them up and threw them into a deep sinkhole.

Those watching at NASA and at C and L Automation yelled in unison: "Nooooo!"

Annihilation of a Planet II

The whirlwind seemed to follow them down into the sink hole, drilling down, closing in the sides of the hole until there was no remnant of the hole in which Spirit and Android Three were buried. The back bed attached to the module was ripped off as, simultaneously a larger whirlwind threatened to bear down on the remaining crew. Those watching via TV saw only the spinning picture taken by the camera mounted on the back bed, being carried away by the dust-filled whirlwind.

There was no time to probe the ground to determine a safe detour. Anna McClure motioned for the commander to lead the crew to the left.

"Are you sure?" Harris asked. McClure nodded. "This way!" shouted Harris. Anna was an experienced navigator who had surveyed and studied every map of Mars. Harris knew he could trust her instincts. She turned her team to the side to go around the mini tornado of red dust, and in fifteen minutes they reached the shuttle. The door opened automatically as the three astronauts and two androids carrying Lawrence ran in. The door closed behind them, and cameras came on automatically, allowing the world to see that they were safe.

"Whooooo!" McClure yelled. "We did it! Captain Harris, you are the bomb!"

"What's the matter with you, woman?" Diaz asked. "You using an old phrase like that to define our captain? He is too superior for that!"

Harris laughed. "Stop it guys. You were great! You're a wonderful team. Every person was integral to the effort."

McClure and Diaz high-fived, and the androids looked at each other. "I will never understand this hand-slapping gesture," Android One said.

"It seems to denote great pleasure and accomplishment," Android Two replied, "but in itself it accomplishes nothing."

"Prepare to launch," Harris said as he pressed a button and the ground around the craft began to tremble. The craft lifted, and rocket boosters propelled them into space. The red planet appeared to shrink as the craft traveled at nano speed.

One day of the mission had passed. The trip home would be lengthened to two days so tests could be run enroute. During those two days, tests were performed on the craft and crew. Results showed no alien contaminants were aboard; Lawrence was going home at last.

Entry into the earth's atmosphere was negotiated through a wormhole with no turbulence. Although NASA was established in 1958, its precursor existed in Philadelphia in 1943 when scientists accidentally found—through trial and error—three portals that led into wormholes. These had been used for the moon and Mars mission explorations over the past decades. Gone was the need of heat shields; a sonic boom on entry was also a thing of the past. The craft smoothly landed on the tarmac at Cape Canaveral, Florida, as

Annihilation of a Planet II

media drones buzzed around like small birds trying to capture the best photographs of this great event.

Zig Fletcher was on the scene. "Ladies and gentlemen, the Bird of the Universe—Yu Yan—has landed. If you will recall, as we reported only after the early launch of this craft, Dr. Paul Linsdale named this project Yu Yan after the ancient Ming dynasty vase he sold to help pay for the mission." The camera shifted from Fletcher to the aircraft.

"Present today is the President of the United States and several of his cabinet," Fletcher continued in a voice over, "as are family members and invited guests. Thousands from around the world are watching on television sets, computers and wrist devices."

The sound of the crowd's loud cheering interrupted the reporter. "Let's watch what is happening," Fletcher said.

The hatch opened and the three astronauts walked out, holding their helmets at their side, waving and smiling broadly. The crowd responded with chants.

"U.S.A.! U.S.A.! Earth is here to stay!"

"A united way with the U.S.A.!"

Protestors with signs reading "Mankind first" had been relieved of their posters. No signs were allowed among the crowd.

A college precision marching band with trumpets and drums began a show, performing on a section of tarmac reserved for them. As the three astronauts reached the president, the band ended its performance amid cheers and applause from the crowd.

Zig Fletcher's face came back on television screens around the world. "Global News Network is here live at Cape Canaveral, where the Yu Yan mission has just been completed. Astronauts Tim Harris, Anna McClure and Berto Diaz have approached the president. An outstanding performance by the University of Alabama's precision marching band has moments ago greeted these three heroes and entertained the crowd. Let's watch as the astronauts meet the president."

The crowd and television audience watched as Tim Harris took off his gloves and shook hands with the president. The two men paused and looked at the cameras for a still shot that would be beamed around the world. Astronauts McClure and Diaz stood by, smiling, showing their delight to be part of this historic occasion.

The reporter's voice was heard once again by the television audience. "What a moment! Everyone will remember what he or she was doing at the time this happened."

The camera again panned toward the air craft. The landing bay hatch opened, and out came the stellar module, driven by one of the androids. On a back bed, the remaining android was holding onto the body of Lawrence as the vehicle approached the president. Over the scene came Fletcher's voice. "Here is the vehicle that carried our heroes over the terrain on Mars, although the back bed is different. This team was ultra-prepared. They had no way of

Annihilation of a Planet II

knowing the first back bed would be blown away on Mars, but here they are, back on Earth with a back bed on which to carry Lawrence with dignity. As all of you must know by now, one android was lost in a sandstorm near the end of the mission on the red planet, as was the newly discovered NASA twin rover Spirit, which was lost for the first time in 2010. We do not know what information may have been gathered from Spirit before it was lost once again in a whirlwind of red dust."

The vehicle stopped in front of the president, and he examined the body of Lawrence. As he did so, Fletcher resumed his commentary. "Remember, this is the president whose motto is, "We must conquer space before it conquers us ... as it conquered the dinosaurs."

The president stepped back and gave a thumbs up. The crowd cheered as the president and his entourage made their way back to Air Force One. At the top of the steps at the door of the plane, he turned and waved again.

"There you have it, ladies and gentlemen, a scene for the ages. I'm Zig Fletcher for GNN ... and I see the astronauts walking this way. Let me see if I can get a word with them before they get into the helicopter taking them to their debriefing. ... Tim! Tim Harris! May I have a word with you, sir?"

The stellar module was being loaded into the bay of the helicopter when Tim heard his name called. Anna and Berto were still waving to the crowd when Tim walked over to Zig.

"Hello, Zig," Tim said, shaking his hand.

Zig's joyful surprise that Tim knew his name made him think of soaring ratings.

"Tim, you were the lead astronaut on this mission. You faced some hair-raising moments there on the planet Mars, and I have to tell you, the world was watching. You had me and my audience on the edge of our seats! You kept your cool and formulated plans right on the spot to bring your crew home safely."

"Zig, I thank you for that, but I couldn't have done it without my team. Berto Diaz is the best computer linguist around, and his contribution cannot be overestimated. And Anna McClure ... well, without Anna's expertise in Mars topography, we never would have made it back to the ship through those red whirlwinds."

"Man, that was something," Fletcher replied. "Red whirlwinds, dirt devils, sink holes, dangerous terrains, and almost being blinded by the old rover Spirit! No one could make this stuff up! And all to get back one humanoid."

Tim Harris turned from Zig and looked straight into the camera, his eyes bold and unblinking. "We humans have no fear of danger. We look danger in the eye, and we say, 'Let's rock!'" His brows drew close together to show his intensity.

Unbeknownst to anyone, Lawrence's inner components became activated for a split second, just

Annihilation of a Planet II
long enough for him to hear the words, "Let's rock."
Then the components went dead again.

The crowd watching the interview on a big screen at Cape Canaveral cheered and shouted their approval as Tim moved to join Anna and Berto, who were walking quickly to the U.S. Navy helicopter to climb aboard. Pausing at the top of the steps, they turned to the crowd, smiling and waving like Hollywood celebrities before ducking under the doorway and disappearing inside. The entire scene was captured by cameras of news outlets from around the world—among them the cameras of Global News Network.

As the helicopter lifted off, Zig Fletcher's face once again appeared on the GNN screen. "There you have it, ladies and gentlemen! We humans, when faced with danger, must pull ourselves together and say in confidence, 'Let's rock!' I am so proud to be an American and a citizen of the world. This is Zig Fletcher at Cape Canaveral Space Center, signing off for GNN."

Fletcher smiled until the red light on the camera went off, then high-fived the cameraman. "My ratings are going to go through the roof, man!" His entire crew were shouting and patting each other on the back except for the one cameraman who was capturing the exit of the U.S. Navy helicopter escorted by two Apache helicopters, making its way to Dr. Paul Linsdale's lab, where a team of scientists were ready to restore Lawrence.

7

Surprise and Deception

On the flat roof of the Computerized & Laboratory Automation building, a white-coated team awaited the helicopters. As the navy aircraft set down with its big rotors whirling, the scientists' hair was tossed around, matching their heart rates and emotions at this great undertaking. The astronauts came out, laughing and shaking hands, first with Dr. Linsdale and then with team members. Paul gave two thumbs up and shouted, "Mission accomplished!" as the two androids came out of the bay carrying Lawrence on a stretcher.

The astronauts turned to get back on the helicopter, bound for NASA to undergo debriefing. "Thank you for your service!" Linsdale called to them. "You have no idea what a great deed you have done for your country. Only the future will inform you of the significance of your work on this mission."

Annihilation of a Planet II

The navy craft rose to join the Apaches hovering above, and the three helicopters took off for Houston.

Paul turned his attention to the androids. "I am sorry about the loss of Android Three. His death was not in vain."

The androids looked down, not understanding this expression of sympathy. Only Lawrence and the Cybernauts that had been destroyed had been embedded with the ability to understand emotions. Paul's father's death had meant the end of that technology. Android One simply said, "Thank you," an expression programmed in as a response for such gestures.

A force field around the roof was keeping news drones away as the androids carried Lawrence into the building and into a lab especially prepared for him.

A man in his fifties continued to watch the TV screen he had darkened with his remote as soon as the news was over and he had seen Lawrence carried onto the U.S. Navy helicopter. Deep in thought, he recalled a day as a teenager, remembering his own encounter with Lawrence. A tear rolled down his cheek. Brian Gates now operated a security company and owned youth centers across the country. He was seated in the office of his security company.

"Randy, take over, will you? I'm leaving you in charge of operations—calling it a night."

"Not feeling well, Brian?"

"No, I'm fine. I have a lot on my mind right now," Brian replied as he moved toward the door. Walking outside and looking up at the stars, he vowed to go visit his old humanoid friend, Lawrence, once he was restored. Lawrence would remember him. He had to! He knew Lawrence would be pleased to know about the work he did with underprivileged youths. If not for Lawrence, Brian's life and ambition would have taken a dramatically different turn.

As Brian walked out of his office, a TV monitor in the lobby was playing the news. A picture of Mother Teresa and Princess Diana caught his eye, and he stopped to watch and listen.

"In today's news, drones are now being used to sweep away landmines, and the event is being dubbed 'The Mother Teresa, Princess Diana Project.' The picture you see on your screen of the two women together was taken in 1997 in the Bronx, New York, when they began their campaign to remove 110 million landmines that littered the world, causing tragedy, destroying legs and arms," the reporter said.

"These drones can clear acres of earth that have been left unwalked for centuries for fear of landmines," the reporter continued. "One day this land will be safe for development and agricultural use. These drones are even used to pollinate rare flowers in Hawaii's high mountain tops where bees are scarce. In honor of the two women's mission from the 20th century, the locals have given these rare flowers the name '*Zipporah-Mother Teresa-Princess D of Wales.*' It's a mouthful, but the name has become well-recognized."

Annihilation of a Planet II

In the lab, Linsdale and his staff stood around the table looking down at Lawrence, his decaying face and body, beaten and weathered by the Martian climate and windstorms. Paul rubbed his hair back from his forehead in a gesture of dismay.

"We have some serious work to do," one scientist said. There were head nods all around.

"We have only two weeks to get him ready for his appearance, get his mechanical functions going," said another. "The world is watching."

"No pressure there!" quipped yet another, and everyone laughed. "Maybe we should get ol' Zig from GNN up here to give a play-by-play."

Everyone groaned and laughed at the joke.

Linsdale smiled. "I know, people, the pressure is on us, but don't I have the best qualified robotic engineers working for me?"

They all looked at each other and nodded their heads in a unanimous yes. "Right!" they said, cheering.

"Then let's get to work!" Linsdale exclaimed. "Let's put on our operating scrubs and glove up. We'll meet in the O.R. in 15 minutes."

Paul put on light green scrubs and hurried to the O.R. His entire crew was there, dressed in light blue scrubs. These colors were chosen because they made operating movements easier to see, not causing illusion or the macular bleaching white scrubs would have caused, dulling the visual acuity of the operatives.

Lawrence's body had been automatically transported by a cart bed that was computer driven to a spot over a red cross in the middle of the operating room, directly under large operating lights that turned on automatically when the cart was situated beneath it. The doors closed.

"Gloved up, goggles on. Let's begin," Linsdale said, struggling to keep his voice level and professional. "Computer, give me the serial analysis on the airborne bacteria count."

"Calculating," came the response from an overhead speaker. Five seconds later the robotic voice boomed forth: "Fifty-seven percent and rising."

"Put on your face masks," Paul instructed his team. "Now stand away." He pushed a button, and a cold frost of crystal smog shot down from above, reducing visibility to zero for 15 seconds.

Gradually the fog dissipated, and the computer voice announced, "Operating room germ-free."

Almost as one the scientists returned to the table, each two-person team assigned to a different part of Lawrence's body, inserting new parts or removing decayed pieces of his artificial skin. Paul Linsdale and Elizabeth Iceland worked on Lawrence's eyes. They fitted in a new set of indigo blue eyes featuring light rays that beamed out. These would allow Lawrence to see in the dark, but the eyes also had an infrared light for night vision for situations when night perception needed to be altered.

As the two scientists worked, Lawrence's eye balls moved rapidly back and forth in his eye sockets,

Annihilation of a Planet II

zooming in like a high-powered telescope. Paul held an instrument off to the side of Lawrence's sclera to adjust the eyes to the right super focus the humanoid would need. Satisfied with the eyes, Paul nodded to Elizabeth and they manipulated Lawrence's eyebrows the way an ocular plastic surgeon would adjust a human's brows.

Two other two-person teams worked on Lawrence's bionic hands, which began to open and close; suddenly the arms came up and the fingers of one hand touched the fingers of the other hand. There were smiles all around the table. Elbows and knees were bending; wrists and ankles were flexing. Now it was time for the moment of truth, the purpose of the mission. What had happened to that third eye, the pineal gland into which so much memory had been received and stored?

Two tubes, one on each side of Lawrence's head, were connected from the computer through Lawrence's ear canals into his microchip brain. "What is the final repair needed?" Linsdale asked the computer. Seconds later the answer came: "Artificial pineal gland has been damaged. The rods and cones of the ganglion cells are obstructed by a cataract."

A mutter of disappointment went around the table. Taking a deep breath, Linsdale shook his head. *It can't be!* he thought. *That third eye is where all the vital data on the race of aliens are stored. We lost the rover Spirit. We can't lose this, too!* "Computer, reanalyze. Could it be Florentine deposits rather than a cataract?"

"Reanalyzing. ... It's a cataract that has stopped the beacon signal you were receiving."

"Amazing," Paul said, groaning and shaking his head.

The computer had not finished. "By my calculation, if we do not repair his pineal gland he will see upside down, making him unable to convert images to right side up. The continued leakage coming from the pineal gland will cause a chemical imbalance, making him schizophrenic or have some other mental changes."

"The pineal gland made him nearly human," Paul said. "My father was a genius." He thought but did not say, *But to what end? Do we want to create duplicates of humans? We can't play God.*

"There is only one way to fix this problem," Linsdale said. "Computer, start the repair."

Eight miniature, metallic spiders about one millimeter in length began to travel from the computer through the clear tubes that went through Lawrence's ear cavities. The crew stood aside, watching on a large screen that showed the microscopic spider-like robots as though they were the size of tennis balls. The micro-robots skittered into action, swimming through the cerebral plasma fluid to Lawrence's pineal gland. The leakage of the gland was shown on the screen like a crack on a coffee cup. Some of the robotic spiders stretched away any artificial tissue obstructing the work area, their eight legs extended out, stretching like telescopes, longer than their original size. One spider

Annihilation of a Planet II

began to remove the cataract deposits, then sutured around the leaking gland, spinning around and around the whole pineal gland with a tight wrap; the leakage stopped. The spider then made a precision tie, bringing the suture together in a knot as another spider made the final cut of the suture with its mandible. Because spider's silk was five times stronger than steel and yet highly elastic, in normal medical practices it was often used in various types of surgery. With the cut, all eight robotic spiders swam away, back into the inner tubes from Lawrence's ear canals to be suctioned out by the computer and cleaned and sterilized with gas.

"That should do it, team," Dr. Paul announced. "Step one is done. I hope we'll be able to get some important data from Mars, or NASA is not going to be happy with us."

All his colleagues had left for home, but before heading out himself, Paul looked through the window of the O.R., wanting one last look at Lawrence. Feeling a great sense of accomplishment, he watched the monitors for a while, thinking eagerly of the end of the next 72 hours, when Lawrence should be fully functional.

Lawrence lay alone on the table, plugged into monitors that were measuring his vital signs. He was wired into equipment the way a cell phone is plugged in for full charge. The monitor showed his artificial heart beating with his pulse. Slowly, from a flat line state, the monitor moved up to two percent. Paul knew once Lawrence was fully charged, he would never have to be charged again. This process was, literally, bringing him back from the dead.

Lawrence's eyes and skin would thereafter harness Vitamin D from the sun, as humans did. Paul pondered the wonder of God's creation. The sun as a power source was best during the rising sun until the clock struck 11:21 A.M. Any time after that, the sun tone went from white to yellow to orange, then red as it prepared for sunset.

Paul sighed as he turned away, going to the sink to wash his hands. He grabbed two paper towels to dry his hands, then crumbled them and tossed them into a trash can. He muttered a prayer, "Please, God, let this mission of bringing Lawrence back be a success. So much money has been invested in this project." For Paul, however, the Yu Yan project was about much more than money. It was about legacy, hope and information. It was about saving earth from annihilation at the hands of man.

Three days later Linsdale leapt from bed full of hope and anticipation. His homecare android, Charles, brought Paul a cup of coffee as he adjusted the tie on his white dress shirt. Eli walked into the room and smiled, coming up to him to smooth his collar as he sipped his coffee.

"Big day today, Eli!" Linsdale said. "Imagine how much bigger it would be if we had been able to bring the rover Spirit home. All those data … lost!"

"It's never enough, is it?" Eli said.

Annihilation of a Planet II

Not answering, he walked to the window overlooking the pond and gazed at the towering water geyser that shot sprays of water into the air. He wondered why the ground had suddenly swallowed Spirit, and why those red dirt devils suddenly appeared out of nowhere, as if there were a hidden force behind them. Was there something that did not want humans to know what once existed there? ... Or still existed there?

He quickly finished his coffee as Eli came up behind him and reached for his hand. She took the coffee cup from his other hand and set it on the table. "Close your eyes, Paul. Relax." She removed his neck tie and slowly began to unbutton his shirt.

"Eli ... what are you doing? I have no time for this."

"Shhh." She looked at him with soulful eyes.

"But I'm running late as it is."

She pushed him, backing him up onto the bed, shoving him down and lying on top of him. "I know what's best," she whispered as she began to kiss his lips. She paused and looked over her shoulder. "Charles, call Dr. Linsdale's office and let them know he will be running late again this morning."

The android turned to repeat a routine that had become familiar to him over the past month. The woman was set on becoming pregnant, and she seemed to think these morning calls were the way to go about it.

"Oh! Oh, okay, Eli," Paul said, his face, neck and chest covered with her kisses. "You know best how to relax me."

Linsdale was speed walking down the hall to the lab, where his team of scientists was waiting. Paul had changed the code at the door the previous night to make sure no one got in before his arrival, and he could see the impatience on their faces. He combed his fingers through his hair and smiled a hello.

"What took you so long?" Elizabeth asked.

"Ahh ... I was analyzing the Marsquake that took the rover, studying what the riticscale measurement would have read."

"I see," Elizabeth responded. "And I wonder what the riticscale from the love bite on your neck would read."

Blushing, Paul tried to cover it up by tightening his tie and collar. He could see that his team was not amused. There were frowns all around. The best thing to do in this case was to change the subject. Punching in the new code, Linsdale said, "Let's get to work."

Iceland replied, "With pleasure," as she stalked in ahead of him.

He shrugged it off and smiled, knowing once they started working, all the frustrations would be forgotten. They trooped in to where they had left Lawrence, but he was not there. Paul's smile fled as he put his hands on the table. "Where did he go?"

Annihilation of a Planet II

Everyone looked around in panic. What could have happened? They looked in the nearby rooms. No Lawrence.

"Quick, everyone, search the premises! He has to be somewhere in the building!" Linsdale yelled, fear turning his voice an octave higher than usual.

A voice from high in the rafters wafted down. "No need to search for me. I'm up here."

They all looked up to see Lawrence levitating under the high glass ceiling.

"I'm admiring the great blue sky and the rising sun."

With one motion of his hand Lawrence brought Linsdale and his team of 12 scientists up to the ceiling. In slow motion they moved skyward, all of them swinging their arms and legs back and forth, trying to stay upright and keep their balance. The higher they rose, the less flailing their balancing motions became as they grew used to the levitation.

Paul had an amused look on his face, and he winked at Elizabeth Iceland. She relaxed a little, but the other members of the team held onto their tight, frightened expressions. Their heads bobbed as they glanced quickly down and then back up, fearing what would happen if they suddenly fell. When they reached Lawrence they were 38 feet in the air. He was looking out the airgell window pane made of 98% condensed air.

He looked at the team of scientists. "Enjoy the view," he said softly. "Don't be afraid. Look at that beautiful sky."

Instead, Paul was looking at Lawrence, a robot created some 50 years previously by Simon Linsdale. The humanoid had the appearance of an ideal young man, lean and muscular, six-foot, four-inches in height, clean cut with jet black hair, combed to perfection.

"How I have missed seeing the blue sky with cirrus clouds and the warm, bright glow of the sunshine ... so much more pleasing than the bleak red sky with dim sunshine on Mars," Lawrence said. "This sight makes my artificial body feel energized again!"

Paul tried to speak, but at first his nerves choked his voice. He cleared his throat and looked down to the white tile of the floor. Then he looked back at Lawrence. "May I, Dr. Paul Linsdale, the son of the late Dr. Simon Linsdale, welcome you back to earth, Lawrence? It's been nearly 30 years since you were last here on our planet."

Lawrence did not look away from the large dome window as he replied, "Did you say my creator has died?"

"Yes, but he lives in me, now. All his hard studies and innovations to improve mankind live on. My team of scientists and I have brought you home and restored you to your precise, original design."

Annihilation of a Planet II

The team had gotten their bearings by this time, and they began nodding their heads, agreeing with their leader.

"Yes, we sure did."

"We did, indeed."

"That's right."

They were all looking out the window as an eagle flew by, its six-foot wing span nearly covering the window, a fish in its talons. The sight calmed them further, and they felt grateful to be high off the ground to see such a glorious sight.

Lawrence turned to gaze at the scientists. "Look at the grand eagle, the favorite bird of the great spirit, God. Man must be like the eagle. At age 40 the eagle will come to a decision to either allow nature to take its course and shortly die, or rejuvenate itself with vitality to live another 30 years. If it decides to take the second path, it will take flight to a high mountain top. There its aged, straggly body will begin its restoration process. First it will chip its worn, bent beak up against the rock face, back and forth until it breaks off. Slowly a new, bright yellow beak will grow back where the old one once was. Then it will pick away at its old, dull and worn out talons that can no longer kill or hold onto its prey. New talons will grow back, sharp and strong again. Then it will start to pluck off the old feathers from its wings. They have become too heavy for flight, keeping the eagle from soaring high in the sky. New, vibrant feathers will then begin to grow. The eagle, rejuvenated, will take flight again, soaring high above the sky, higher than any other bird can, looking at God's majestic landscape, the greatest planet to be created. I am like this great bird—reconstructed by you, Dr. Linsdale, and your team of scientists." He bowed his head slightly to them as a gesture of gratitude and appreciation.

"First comes creation made by the creator. Then the creature has the ability and capability toward Charles Darwin's natural selection," Lawrence added. He turned back to watch the eagle as it continued to fly on the updrafts, finally becoming a small dot in the distance. "I, too, must fly like an eagle and vanish," he said.

Linsdale's heart began to beat erratically. "But … but you can't! We have invested so much money to bring you back to learn about the lost small colony of aliens that lived on the planet between Mars and Jupiter that is now the asteroid belt. You and the Cybernauts found their study laboratory on Mars, and the information is in your pineal gland!"

"Yes and no," Lawrence replied.

"What? What do you mean?" one of the scientists yelled.

"I have it here," Lawrence said, reaching into his vest pocket and pulling out a shiny, small disc about the size of a quarter and handing it to Linsdale. All the information you seek is here with alien technology. I downloaded it. You can decipher the inscription."

Paul held it gently in his hand, looking at it in excitement mixed with a strange feeling of reverence.

Annihilation of a Planet II

He looked at Lawrence as the robot held out another disk.

"Give this to NASA," the humanoid said. "These mathematical coordinates will shift the Earth's alignment back on its proper axis. They will know what to do. This will keep everyone in the scientific world busy for a while so I can have freedom for my quest. You have your disc, and NASA has a math problem to solve for the sake of the earth." He held out his hand to Linsdale to shake. "Goodbye, now. I must go. I, too, have a mission to complete. I must study and learn about the strongest force in the universe."

"What mission? What force?" Paul asked.

"It is something you humans have and can possess completely if you will only open yourselves to it. It is found in the human heart." With those words Lawrence made a downward motion with one hand, and the scientists slowly began to descend. As they floated toward the ground, they looked up at Lawrence and were astonished as he transformed into light and vanished.

"How did he do that?" Elizabeth Iceland asked.

"We don't have the technology to do that!" another said.

"We need to get him back so we can learn about it," someone else yelled.

"Perhaps it's on the disc he gave us," Linsdale said quietly. "For now, it's what we have."

The feet of all the scientists hit the floor at once, and they were bumping into each other in their hurry to get to their stations to try to process what had just happened.

"Please! Team!" shouted Linsdale. "Let's calm down and regain our composure. Please."

"Wait!" Elizabeth shouted. "We are forgetting something. The media will arrive soon"—she looked at the clock—"in an hour! They expect to see Lawrence."

Groans sounded around the room.

"Change of plans!" Paul shouted. "We have to move quickly. Get an android in here from robotic engineering. We have no time to waste."

From the assembly line they took an almost complete android intended for household use. Linsdale gave instructions to the assembly computer, putting in the binary numbers of Lawrence into the android's artificial brain. The son of the great Simon Linsdale believed he was giving this android the recollection of every aspect of what Lawrence knew so that it could respond to reporters' questions without hesitation. Paul had no way of knowing the binary numbers he transferred were defective. Two days earlier a janitor had knocked over a full coffee cup onto the backup data panel, damaging the microchips. There was no way to know what horrors those defective microchips might bring.

"Dr. Linsdale," the computer said. "I have finished downloading Lawrence II's genetic information."

Annihilation of a Planet II

"Very good. Prepare to sterilize the O.R.," commanded Linsdale. "Everyone adjust facemasks and step back."

Crystal fog shot from above the operating table, covering it and the floor around it. Fifteen seconds later, the computer declared, "Germ free."

Leaving Lawrence II on the table, the scientists rushed toward Linsdale's office to play the alien technology disc. A swarm of reporters stopped the scientists' progress, and Paul quickly put the disc into his pocket.

A reporter stood in front of Paul and thrust a microphone toward his face. "Sir, we have been waiting here for nearly half an hour. Aren't we going to get a progress report today?"

Dr. Linsdale rubbed his forehead and looked at the reporters. "Sure. We have taken lengthy steps to restore Lawrence, and it was a success. My team of scientists have worked long hours by my side."

"Well, will he get full restoration?" another reporter shouted, pushing between two others to get his mic up to Paul's face.

"Yes, he will. We have him in Bay Five, recovering." Paul thought of the android in Bay Five looking nothing like Lawrence except for height. There was still cosmetic work to be done.

"My team and I are exhausted. We are going to call it a day, and the world will see him at the grand opening at the Boston Smithsonian Museum. You'll be able to personally ask him all the questions you desire at that time. For now, my scientists and I have important matters to address."

A third reporter, already at the front of the pack, pushed her mic forward. "We expected to see him today. Did something go wrong?" At her question, other reporters were immediately on the alert, and a dozen microphones were thrust forward.

"No, nothing went wrong," Paul said forcefully. "I assure everyone. It's just boring, detailed information we have to address, dotting the i's and crossing the t's."

Muttering and grumbling, the crowd of reporters left. As soon as they were out of sight, Paul looked furtively to the left and right to make sure he and his team were alone. "Quickly, everyone, follow me to Bay Eleven," he commanded.

They made a mad dash to the lab. With a sigh the double doors automatically opened under a lighted sign that read 'Restricted Area.' Dr. Linsdale pulled the disc from his lab coat pocket and held it up for his crew to see. They gathered around like kids in a candy store as the computer began to download the data. Almost as one they quickly turned to the center of the laboratory, where from the floor base in a 20-foot circle, a three-dimensional image with rays of blue and green light appeared. Alien codes and letterings appeared in the rays as the scientists watched in the otherwise dark room.

Suddenly the skull-like face of an alien appeared at the main center floor, midway in the air; and almost as one, Linsdale's team stepped back a foot.

Annihilation of a Planet II

When the alien began to speak in a low, quiet tone in an unknown language, Dr. Linsdale asked the computer, "Can you decipher what the alien recording is stating?"

After tracking the frequency for a few seconds, the computer responded, "Unable to compute. But the alien data have informed me that Lawrence, in his 30 years on Mars, has been able to crack the code and decipher the language."

"Computer can you do it, too?" asked Dr. Linsdale.

"I can work on it, but it might take me 25 years to do it ... maybe longer."

The looks on the faces of the team members were a mixture of dismay and grief. They bowed their heads, showing they felt completely crushed.

Paul refused to accept defeat. "Okay, computer, go to work on the code. The rest of you, we must try to get the real Lawrence back here someway, somehow ... or we wait 25 years or 30 years. Who knows? I know you're disappointed. So am I. Let's call it a night and go to our loved ones. I could sure use a ..."

He stopped in mid-sentence as he looked at his staff. Instead of speaking further he massaged his head as everyone stared at him. They walked past him to leave, and he heard Elizabeth mutter, "Just please be on time tomorrow morning!" They were all laughing as they walked down the hall.

Antonion Borges

Through the window Paul watched his crew get into their sealanders, and then he walked out as his vehicle came to pick him up. He boarded and lay down on the seat, elevating the pillow slightly.

"Destination, doctor?" the sealander asked.

"Home!"

"Very good, sir" replied the sealander.

"And give me Mozart."

As the soothing music poured forth, the sealander moved at 10 mph to the main Tesla belt, accelerating from 10 to 20 to 100 mph in seconds. Dr. Linsdale poured himself a quick shot of vodka nicely chilled in the sealander's icebox. Musing over the busy day he had with his crew, he wondered where Lawrence could possibly be.

8

Reaping What Was Sown

Mid-afternoon found Lawrence strolling through a prairie, while rabbits nibbled on grass around his feet. He picked up one of the cotton tails and gently stroking the soft fur, whispered into the rabbit's ear, "I am here to express to all God's creation man's purpose for life, why he is here and where he is going, for the word was God."

As the rabbit lay peacefully along his arm, head in hand, Lawrence continued, "The word is God— the transformation into living flesh coming to earth as Jesus to save mankind from destruction. And he will come again to restore heaven and earth as two parallel worlds. Then, as one, the whole world will kneel before him. Suffering, disease and hunger will be no more, and the animals will walk with man as it was before the great flood, during Noah's time."

Bending down and placing the rabbit back on the soft prairie grass among the wild flowers, Lawrence commanded, "Go now and spread the news!" He smiled as he looked up at the honeybees, hard at work collecting pollen for making honey at their hives.

The rabbit hopped away and excitedly rubbed noses with other rabbits before hurrying to a squirrel with his message. He moved on to a turtle and then to a beaver that had a branch in its mouth. The beaver dropped the branch, and standing on his hind legs, looked up at the sky as tears rolled from his eyes. The beaver began nodding his head up and down in excitement as the rabbit circled around him, hopping up and down. Smiling at the rabbit, Lawrence vanished like a beam of light, as quickly as he had appeared.

He reappeared in Israel, the Holy Land, and he found himself in a war of exploding, earth-shaking bombs; billowing smoke filled the air. Women and children were caught in the crossfire. Walking into the midst of the battle, Lawrence emitted a powerful lion's roar, and the soldiers stopped shooting at one another. As the smoke clouds from artillery fire slowly dissipated, soldiers on both sides of the battle could see a tall figure with arms outstretched, standing over a woman and child hunched down and curled up together. Blood streamed down the woman's forehead as she held her child close to her bosom. Mother and child looked frightened as they cried out for God to save them.

"Who's that out there?" yelled the Israeli general, mounted on a tank looking through his binoculars.

Looking on in awe, a warlord commanded a ceasefire as the figure of Lawrence appeared to him as a lion.

Boldly and loudly Lawrence shouted, "God will not condone this bloodshed on his land, the holy of holies! This will be stopped by God's mighty hand! I have come here to pray, and instead I find myself amid utter chaos and horror inflicted by men on one another."

The woman and child remained where they lay, shivering but otherwise unmoving at Lawrence's feet. The woman looked up at his face as Lawrence continued. "God gave land to man to live on it with all his other creations, from the birds that sing to us, to the trees that clean the air and gives us shade from the hot sun. I hear no happy tunes here from birds, nor do I see trees providing shade. Instead it's bombshells and the bloody stench of rotten carcasses. You cannot even see the simplest things in life here, such as the honeybee."

He thought of the honeybees he'd seen in the United States of America, knowing of the crisis that had been averted in the 21st century when the honeybees were nearly eliminated with the overuse of pesticides.

"Watching the honeybees buzz from flower to flower to pollinate the trees and plants, enabling them to have fruit and other edible vegetation, one sees the miracle of the ecosystem—of life. So can the animals and man nourish themselves to sustain life. But what good is life, if it's always in utter chaos? For this land is truly the dwelling place of God.

Christians, Jews and Muslims come here to pray. Lay down your arms and seek another place for your wars if you must. Leave God's house and land of milk and honey to be a place of sovereign sanctuary! Do this for God the most high, so that peace will be restored here!"

A loud, thunderous bolt of lightning raced across the sky. All became silent as the soldiers looked up at the sky filled with racing clouds. Finally there came a shout, "Is that a warning from high above?"

"Take it as you wish," Lawrence replied, "for God will rain down here a series of plagues, just as he did on the ancient Egyptians during the time of Pharaoh Ramses! For do not, I urge you, test the will of God, the Almighty One, as Pharaoh unfortunately did. Moses gave him full warning before every plague that was to come if he did not let His people go from bondage. Ramses chose to ignore the warnings."

An Israeli commander yelled out to Lawrence, "We want to live in peace, but the Palestinians constantly raid our towns and schools with suicide bombers!"

A Palestinian yelled out, "We have no choice! We have harmed those who protest their innocence while living on land taken from us. The Israelis keep expanding territory, claiming what is ours as their own. Our peoples once lived here side-by-side, from the times of the mighty Samson and King Saul, King David, King Solomon. We've migrated here since the fifth century BC from the Mediterranean islands of Greece, coming here by way of the Aegean Sea to

Annihilation of a Planet II

live among the Israelites. We, too, seek peace. We want to keep our roots here, as we have done since King Achish of Gath of 290 BC, in what is known as the Gaza Strip. It is part of the Arab nations."

"Can we not break bread together?" Lawrence asked, looking from one to the other of the opposite forces. "I know of this King Achish of Gath, which was one of the five cities of Philistia—now modern day Palestine. It was to Gath that the young David fled under the prophet Samuel's warning that King Saul was on the hunt for his head. When David was brought to King Achish, David was in fear for his life, for he had killed the Gath giant Goliath three years previously. Knowing the king might now take revenge, David pretended to be a mad man, insane in their presence."

Although everyone on the battlefield had heard this story, the field was silent as Lawrence told it. He caused a hologram to appear from the sky so that everyone could see it. The two armies stared at the scene in which the king was sitting in his rich, lofty chamber, seated in his royal chair. As David was led in, the musicians abruptly stopped playing their harps and flutes. Two guards held spears at David, waiting for the king's command to kill him. Guests and members of the court sat at richly appointed tables, entertained by this intrusion. Some young women, nibbling at grapes and dried figs, laughed at the appearance of the so-called giant slayer.

In the hologram, Achish looked at David in disgust. "Isn't this the future King of Israel, to whom they danced and sang?"

"Yes, your Majesty," the principal slave replied. "It went like this: 'Saul has slain his thousands and David his tens of thousands.'" With a broad smile on his face, the slave burst into song. "Saul has slain his thousands and David his tens of thousands."

All the court singers joined in, repeating the words over and over, and the dancers swayed and stepped to the music.

"Enough! Stop that nonsense this instant," yelled the King. He shook his head in disgust. "Look at the man! He is insane!" roared Achish. "Why bring him to me? Am I so short of madmen that you have to bring this fellow here to carry on like this in front of me?" David, with saliva drooling down his beard, pretended to write with his fingers on the walls. "Take him away from me and release him out of the territory at once."

Lawrence spoke. "And so it happened that David was released, and with his crushed, humiliated spirit he ran to a cave and prayed to God that he would never again allow his pride to override himself."

At this moment the hologram closed, and again all eyes were upon Lawrence. He said, "The wisdom of this humility that David showed was to set aside his pride. It is pride that separates us from God and from one another. That's why God opposes it."

"Who are you?" a voice from the crowd asked.

"I am Lawrence!"

Immediately there was an uproar as everyone began talking and shouting at once.

Annihilation of a Planet II

"It's Lawrence, who saved us from the mega bomb."

All the soldiers dropped their weapons and walked closer to him. One seemingly spoke for all of them when he said, "We all know this is truly the place of faith, God's holy land."

Lawrence replied, "You must learn from David and put your pride aside in order to accomplish things together. You must all question yourselves. Would it not please God that you all came together in Israel to pray instead of quarrelling with much bloodshed? Who suffers more? The elderly, the women and the children. The Philistines in the Old Testament kept their border, and the Israelites kept their respected land."

Looking down, Lawrence helped up the woman and child from the ground. The woman gazed at Lawrence and said, "Thank you kindly for saving us. My name is Loftus. This is my son Ishmael. My people from the East have migrated here, too, long ago from the Islamic lands."

Lawrence picked up the boy and set him on his shoulders so all could see him, a frightened, shy child with dark hair and brown skin marred with dirt and soot covering his soiled clothing and face. Once again a hologram descended from the sky, this one showing the brothers Ishmael and Isaac. Lawrence spoke, louder and stronger. "Abraham had two children, Ishmael and Isaac. Ishmael from Hagar and Isaac from Sarah, Abraham's wife. He loved both sons and taught them how to hunt and worship the only living God, YHVH. When Abraham died years later, Ishmael received word and stopped everything he was doing so he could journey back to the land where his brother resided. When the two laid eyes on one another after so long a time, they embraced in a tearful hug."

A murmur went through the crowd as Muslims and Jews acknowledged their common heritage. Lawrence continued, "In Hebron, among a large gathering of family members that had traveled on camels from both sides, the two men buried their father at the Cave of Machpelah. 'Peace be with you, my brother, Isaac.' 'And peace be with you my brother, Ishmael.' Those were their words as the two embraced in loving memory of their father, born a rich man, leaving everything he had from the land of Ur to follow God's teaching and to give birth to two nations we know of today—the people of Israel and the people of the Muslim nations. For centuries they lived far apart as neighbors in peace."

The scene slowly faded like the mist of early morning disappearing with the sun. All eyes were on Lawrence.

Lawrence continued his history lesson, seemingly in a daze, not aware of his listeners at all, yet still holding Ishmael on his shoulder. "In the beginning was the word, and the word was God, and the word became flesh and made his dwelling among us. We have seen his glory of the one and only Son, who was appointed from the Father, full of grace and truth. His name is Jesus, who is the Word! Before Adam and Abraham. He is the Son of Man! Respect this place of holy ground. For the Father and Son from

Annihilation of a Planet II

heaven above, the eyes can see. Ishmael is the progenitor of many Arabs—both Muslims and Christians. Isaac is the progenitor of the Jews. Not all Muslims are Arabs. There are Israeli Muslims, Persian [Iranian] Muslims, English Muslims, and African Muslims. The Sare Muslims are descendants of Isaac. God never ordained any wrongs against Ishmael and his descendants. He blessed Ishmael and did not curse him! He said he would make of Ishmael a great nation, which he has for both the children of Israel and the Arab nations. They all came from one father, Abraham. They must work together for peace.

The Israeli soldiers all began to cheer loudly, "Ishmael! Ishmael! Ishmael!" clapping their hands and stomping their boots on the ground.

The group of Muslims started chanting "Isaac! Isaac! Isaac!" clapping their hands and stomping their shoes on the ground.

An Israeli man yelled out, "May God bless the descendants of Ishmael!"

An Arab man shouted, "May God bless the descendants of Isaac!"

Back and forth it went, like a song rising high into the air that could be heard for miles, "Isaac! Ishmael! Isaac …! Ishmael!"

The boy on Lawrence's shoulders, hearing his name raised in cheerful song, began to wipe tears from his face. A grand smile seemed to brighten the sky—as if the sun had vanquished all the doom and gloom. As the child waved both hands in the air very fast to both sides, Lawrence looked up at him and gave him a smile. Putting the boy back in his mother's open arms, Lawrence walked with her to the Israeli soldiers, who immediately gave them water to drink and food to eat. Two soldiers took soft cloths and wiped the faces of the mother and child. Both armies laid down their weapons and clasped hands with members of the heretofore opposing side, no longer with closed fists, but with open arms as Ishmael and Isaac had done a long time previously in an ancient world.

As the Muslims and Jews embraced in friendship, feeling the years of social injustice, rage and fear melt away, Lawrence was no longer there. He reappeared in Tabgha, Israel, at a church named the Multiplication of Loaves and Fishes, which centuries earlier had been torched by arsonists. Standing in front of the church entrance stood a priest, who could hear from miles away the enchanting song carrying in the wind: "Ishmael! Isaac!"

Seeing Lawrence, the priest called out, "Come on in for prayer, lonely traveler! What a day to rejoice in prayer to the Lord. Rather than hearing bombshells going off, I hear sweet music from afar! What is your name?"

"Lawrence."

"What country are you from?"

"The United States of America."

"God bless the U.S.A.!" the priest said, clasping his hands together. He put a hand on Lawrence's shoulder and walked him into the church. They stopped inside the entrance and the priest prayed,

"But they shall sit under their own vines and under their own fig trees, and no one shall make them afraid."

They stood in silent prayer for a moment, then Lawrence looked at the old priest and said, "I recognize that prayer. It is from the Bible. It was one of the favorite verses of America's first president. George Washington mentioned it in at least 50 of his letters."

"Tell me, my son," the priest said, "when we prayed silently, for what did you pray?"

"I prayed for the gift of understanding about love and God's creation and plan."

"A noble prayer, but I think you must have prayed for something more," the priest said, looking straight into Lawrence's eyes.

Lawrence smiled. "Yes. I prayed that I would find my long-lost love, Lilah, so we may live till the end of time under our own vines and under our own fig trees."

"Ah! You are in love!"

Lawrence tilted his head and looked at the priest quizzically.

The priest laughed. "And you don't even know it!"

Lawrence nodded and asked, "What is your name?"

"I am Simeon, named from the Bible's Simeon the Elder."

Lawrence and Simeon sat down to talk, and the android spoke of the Simeon of old. "He holds the key to the birth of Christ!"

"Yes, replied the priest. "The Holy Spirit was upon him. God promised him that he would not die until the promised Messiah, Christ the Lord, came into the world."

Lawrence nodded and continued the story. "One day the righteous elder received word from the Holy Spirit that he should go to the temple. He was standing inside the temple with Anna the prophetess, waiting and watching everyone who came in. They saw Mary and Joseph with a baby boy. Simeon asked if he might hold the child, and Mary gladly gave the old man the infant to hold."

The priest smiled at Lawrence and recited the history. "With the Christ child in his hands, Simeon shouted so that everyone could hear, 'Lord, now lettest thou thy servant depart in peace, according to thy word, for mine eyes have seen thy salvation, which thou hast prepared before the face of all people, a light to enlighten the gentiles, and the glory of thy people of Israel.' Shortly after, on that very same day—40 days after Christ's birth—Simeon the righteous passed away peacefully according to the will of God."

"And that is why the date of Simeon's death would give man the true date in time as related to Christ's birth," Lawrence added.

"You are well read, my friend," the priest said. "Our modern day calendar is off by a few years or

Annihilation of a Planet II

even up to five years at the most. Pope Gregory XIII, back in the sixteenth century, commissioned a monk by the name of Dionysius Exiguus to come up with a modern day calendar based on the birth of Christ to replace the Julian calendar, but Dionysius was off by several years. His system did not take into account the zero years. His method went from 1BC to 1AD. If the tomb of Simeon could be found so that the month, day and year of his death were established, then man could count back 40 days to the Law of Moses: 'That every women that bears the first born son must come with an offering to the temple where both are to receive cleansing and blessing.'"

The priest smiled. "Time to rewind the clock." Benjamin Franklin welcomed the change during his time when it was changed from the Julian calendar to the Gregorian calendar," Lawrence said. "Franklin wrote, 'It is pleasant for an old man to be able to go to bed on September 2 and not have to get up until September 14 in the year 1752.'"

The priest laughed loudly.

In Paul Linsdale's lab, news reporters swarmed into the entranceway to capture on film and in words the re-introduction of Lawrence. They had no way of knowing they would be looking at the alpha decoy Lawrence. Linsdale and his team of scientists stood with the facsimile as Paul told the lie: "Here is the anticipated man machine the world has been waiting for! I give you Lawrencium B12, Lr103. This is the name my late father gave him, calling him by that element, but the world knows him as Lawrence." He was founded and named after the great Ernest Lawrence.

The fake Lawrence stood tall, staring at the crowd quietly. Questions were thrown at him all at once. Without skipping a beat, his bionic jaw opened and he began to speak, answering all the questions at once. A human would have asked them to please ask questions one at a time, but not Lawrence II. The answers came out of his mouth so quickly the reporters couldn't keep up. Some questions were repeated, and Lawrence answered them again with the same words and same inflections he had used previously.

"Do you have the mathematical formula to the mega bomb?" a reporter shouted.

Silence spread among the reporters hungry for information. Dr. Elliot leaned against his boss's ear and whispered, "We failed to ask the real Lawrence that question, due to the excitement about the alien disc!"

"Not now, Jimmy," Paul whispered back. "Keep your composure."

"No, I do not!" the robot answered after what seemed like long minutes but, in truth, was only a few seconds. "I was assigned only to take it to Yellowstone National Park, which has the largest underground volcano in the world. I was not given any further orders, but I knew, placed there, the bomb would end the earth as we knew it. The purpose was complete annihilation of this planet! Three decades ago, due to my actions, the mega

Annihilation of a Planet II

bomb was, instead, the source of the Cosmonauts' destruction."

"Good," a woman in the front row of reporters said as she took a deep breath and exhaled in unison with many others. "We certainly don't have to worry about that!" The decoy Lawrence grinned at them with a sinister expression that made them all feel uneasy.

"Where does he go from here, Dr. Linsdale?" another reporter asked.

"He will be property of the New Smithsonian Museum of Science, which is opening its doors in Boston, Massachusetts, tomorrow. We believe Lawrence's presence will generate revenue of $10,000 a week. A percentage of that money will be used here to fund future projects."

Zig Fletcher stepped forward, away from the other reporters, a microphone in his hand. He motioned for his cameraman to get into position for a better shot of him confronting Linsdale. "I just received breaking news from our GNN satellite headquarters in Israel and Palestine," he said. "Lawrence is said to have appeared some hours ago amid a hostile crossfire, saving a Palestinian woman and her child. Further, GNN has learned that agreements for a ceasefire are at hand because of what this Lawrence did."

Paul Linsdale's face turned white, and he stepped back away from the microphone Fletcher had thrust in his face.

"What do you have to say, professor?" Zig continued, pressing forward. "According to this news, Lawrence has effected negotiations and talks for peace and sovereignty, and now high officials and dictators are coming back to the peace table. Are you still contending that we are in the presence of Lawrence, savior of the world?"

Shoving Fletcher's microphone away from Paul's face, Jim Elliot stepped in front of Fletcher. Elliot raised his hands and brought them down slowly to quiet the stream of questions and speculation of the reporters. "Yes, it's true!" Elliot said. "Hours before you came here, we received word of this event. We do not know who the imposter is in the Middle East, but we will be taking full action to stop it. Lawrence does not have the ability to transport his monocular amino acids."

By this time, Linsdale had recovered from his shock. He patted Elliot on the shoulder in thanks and said to the reporter, "I thank you all for coming today. Be assured that we will track down the false Lawrence and find out what his purpose might be. In closing, I'll remind you that we have a big day tomorrow when we transport Lawrence to the new Science Museum."

"Well, who do you think that android is—the one that has brought peace to the Middle East?" asked a young man who was looking to earn his tough-guy stripes in the world of journalism.

"In due time we will find out!" Elizabeth Iceland said as the rest of the team followed Paul and Lawrence II out of the hall. She stood facing the

Annihilation of a Planet II

reporters as her colleagues disappeared, then she herself turned and walked away. Watching her leave, the reporters grumbled and quarreled among themselves. The young reporter muttered, "I smell a fish." He led a few lingering reporters down the hall in the direction the scientists and the robot had taken, but they were stopped at a barrier and an electric sign that read: 'Off Limits. Official Personnel Only. Intruders will be prosecuted.'

Linsdale had nearly fallen into his chair when he got to his office. His heart was beating wildly, and the control he had shown in his final statement had fled. Elizabeth got a glass and filled it from the water cooler, handing it to Paul. He took it gratefully and gulped down half the contents.

"Wow, that was close," Linsdale said to his team of scientists. "We know the decoy we created does not have the ability to transport himself, and neither does any other android. That secret died with my father at his lab. Only one Cybernaut has that ability: Lawrence. We are the only ones who know that for certain. I have yet to configure the lost code of my father's genius mind. I have been unable to replicate Lawrence's specialized flexible skin that allows Lawrence to go into the deep sea and not damage a circuit, keeping it as dry as the Sahara desert!"

Paul shook his head and sighed. He turned to Elizabeth. "You've been studying the synthetic skin, Dr. Iceland. Any progress, yet?"

"No, sir. We've come up with nothing, yet," she said nervously.

Glaring at her, Paul did not try to hide his bad mood. "Someone get me a vitamin stick!"

Jim Elliot quickly gave his boss the requested supplement and Paul began puffing on it right away. Water vapor filled the air as Paul inhaled and exhaled, looking a little more relaxed. "I will have to study it with you personally, then, Elizabeth. As you well know, my time is limited, due to my having to appear at functions to raise money for our company. My name brings in money because it's considered to be a corporate name."

Elizabeth bowed her head, unused to seeing this side of Paul. He was usually so optimistic and upbeat, and she realized he had been deeply shocked to be caught out in the middle of a subterfuge. Dishonesty was completely foreign to Paul, and he was having a difficult time handling the cognitive dissonance combined with the real Lawrence's very public activities.

One scientist giggled and whispered to Iceland, "We better get on the ball or it's off with our heads."

Elizabeth shrugged off her friend. "Don't laugh. This is serious."

Linsdale spoke again. "Now let's get Lawrence II into the refurbishing cylinder so he is well energized for tomorrow's big event!" He stormed out, "I'm calling it a day."

9
Saving a Rainforest

Unaware—and unconcerned—about what might be happening to his friends at Computerized & Laboratory Automation, Lawrence next appeared in a Brazilian rainforest. The Amazonian rainforest, once the oxygen factory of the earth, no longer provided unlimited clean air for the world to breathe fresh air from the troposphere. Rare plants and insects of all kinds once flourished here, but deforestation had changed all that. At one time Brazil's rainforest encompassed an area twice the size of India; it was the largest rainforest on Earth. Now the rainforest had dwindled to the size of Turkey. Lawrence knew if the deforestation continued, the forest would be reduced one day to the size of a U.S. state park.

Many indigenous people had fled their homes and way of life to look for jobs in the concrete jungle built by man. Some of these people were unable to learn urban skills, and they were reduced to panhandling for money, morning and night, to feed their children. The know-how of a proud culture depending on a simple life had been reduced to poverty by modern man. A people that once lived a simple life, depending on vegetation provided in the forest, had been forced away by the urban ones—men who valued gold, diamonds and minerals above the natural riches provided by the rainforest. When asked why in God's name this should continue, the cover-up answer was the need for more open land for cattle. Putting beef on the table had become important. The industrialized world's tractors and bulldozers demolished any village that got in its way.

Lawrence appeared near the front line of a convoy of tractors making its way to a nearby village. He stared down from a deep forest area on a hill looking over some exotic plants where possible traces of gold has been found. The only trees left standing were palm trees. Other trees, even those decades old, had been destroyed to make room for more palm trees that would be cultivated for their oil. The very old palm trees plundered for their hearts would consequently die, making room for more young trees. The fruit produced by these trees generated oil—a big business in a world in which palm oil was used in close to 50% of household products. Palm oil was highly regarded for use in everything from drinks, sweets and food to paper, fertilizer and detergents. Now rain forests were being destroyed for the planting of palm trees, which had become a cash crop. The companies had used up the natural resources, and their greed to obtain more led them to destroy all other vegetation in order to plant more palm trees.

Annihilation of a Planet II

A band of Titis monkeys looked with curiosity at Lawrence from a treetop branch. Monkeys stood up and down the branch, while others were hanging with one hand on the branch with human-like expressions on their faces. Seeing them, Lawrence remembered his old friend Larf, the laboratory study ape, who had died for the rights of animals, no matter what species they were, because they were all connected in the circle of life.

Knowing the tractors were on their way to destroy their village, a tribe of Indians had begun to dance in full leather gear in front of the tractors to try to stop them from beginning their path of destruction. Some women, with tears rolling down their cheeks, held babies in their arms. They wore native costumes and ornaments made from seashells and turquoise stones. One man stood on a tractor that was soon to make its way into their village of dry grass huts. The tractor stopped, and so did the convoy of 22 other tractors.

The lead tractor driver wiped his forehead and neck with a hand towel. His hand trembled slightly as he yelled out in Portuguese, "You must all leave. This area is now government owned." Pointing to an area miles away that had been destroyed by tractors the previous year, he said, "You must find refuge elsewhere." The landscape he indicated was nothing but red soil and rock.

A chief resplendent in feathers walked up to the man standing on the tractor. The Indian's eyes and voice were cold as he asked, "Have you not taken enough of our ancestral land? How much more must you take from our people for your cattle and palm oil that is grown only here in our precious rainforest? Our tribes need the forest for food and medicine."

The man on the big tractor puffed away at a cigar and wiped the sweat from his forehead. As though he hadn't heard the chief, he took off his hat and extracted a small canister of whiskey from the band. After taking a quick, quenching drink from it, he carefully twisted the cap back on and put it back in his hat before placing the hat on his head. Only then did he look the chief in the eye.

"And who are you that I must respectfully listen?"

Some of the tribe members yelled out, "He is our chief! Guy Sagamor!"

Echoing their words, the chief said, "I am Chief Sagamor. My people have been here for more than 11,000 years. We came from North America!" He looked coldly at the man on the tractor. "And who are you?"

"You can call me Carper. Look, chief, I'm sorry, but I have my orders to complete this job without delay. I cannot break my contract or I'll lose wages of thousands of dollars for me and my men. My business would be gone. Who would then put food on my table and on the tables of the families of my men?"

"You can fulfill other contracts to build cities, homes and sports arenas," Chief Sagamor responded. "My people and I have no place to go if you do this deed. All we want is to live off the land as we've

Annihilation of a Planet II

been doing for thousands of years. My people are lost in your world of technology. We want no part of it."

"This conversation is going nowhere! You were given a 90-day notice to move from here. You and most of your people chose to stay. The smart ones have moved to our cities."

"So I have heard," said the chief, "where they have lost their dignity and now beg for food and water, when once upon a time they lived in their own land of plenty. Your people drove them out."

"That is not true. They are not all beggars. Look, we have one of your people here." He looked back, searching. "There!" He pointed at the fifth tractor back and returned his gaze to the chief. "We have taught him how to operate a tractor, and he's making money! Wait, I will call for him!" Carper again turned and yelled, "Ben! Ride up here."

A tractor turned out of line and came forward. Smoke rose from the tractor's smoke shaft with the powerful sound and the acrid odor of diesel fuel still used in these particular models. The driver reached up and parked his tractor alongside his boss and turned off the ignition. The chief looked to see who it was. With a sad face, Chief Sagamor began to cry in pain. The other Indians began to sing in anguish, kneeling on the ground, throwing soil on their heads and bodies in a sign of defeat. The air was filled with a ritual Indian song of grief.

On the tractor was the chief's eldest son, who was to become chief after Sagamor passed away. A man wearing a white shirt was on the tractor with the young Indian. He stood up as Carper sat down. The man standing was one of the CEO bank investors who had joined the crew to see the land in which he had invested. Lawrence was still standing out of sight behind a tall tree, and he continued to listen to both sides like the old man in the moon, listening to men from afar since the dawn of time.

The Indian man who had driven the tractor forward stood beside the white investor. "Father, it is I! Sparrow Hawk. Forgive me, but I see no future for our people here anymore."

The Indians stopped bathing in the dirt, stopped throwing the soil and dirt on their heads and bodies as a sign of pain and sorrow for Mother Earth and for themselves. They looked up to Sparrow Hawk and became quiet.

"You were the promise to our people, the hope to our people," the chief said to his eldest son. "We've been searching for you, scouting the land day and night, thinking that a jaguar or 'gator was the cause of your nonexistence to us. But now I see that it is far, far worse. Modern man has devoured you instead, into their world of trial and error. How many more mistakes will they make before they realize they have tilted the balance of life?"

Sagamor waved his arms toward the heavens. "The birds of the sky no longer have the ability to migrate, for they are unable to pick up the Great Spirit's invisible force, the earth's magnetic field. Once upon a time the migrating birds' beaks were

Annihilation of a Planet II

used for more than eating and grooming and killing prey. Long ago their bills worked like a needle on a compass with which they navigated toward distant areas for plentiful insects and budding plants. Many flew in V-shaped flocks, all pointing their compass needles toward their destination."

Sparrow Hawk tried to imagine what it must have been like, with birds filling the air, flying to distant locations. This was something he had never seen and only had heard about it from his elders. Tears came to his eyes, and he jumped down from the tractor, a drop of 12 feet.

"The same thing has happened to animals of the ocean," the old chief continued. "Sea lions that once used their whiskers to migrate to distant rocky shores now beach themselves in remote, hostile areas, simply because the Great Spirit's invisible force has been displaced in the seas, just as it has shifted in the sky."

Sagamor rushed forward to put a hand on the young man's shoulder. "Son, you know we have no gold or diamonds here. What we have here is a rich life of other things—bountiful food—game, vegetation, fruits and berries."

Sparrow Hawk bowed his head. "Father and my people, forgive me. I left only to try to negotiate with their leaders, for I am one of the few from our tribe who can speak their language. I tried to reason with them, but I failed." Suddenly he straightened and looked the CEO in the eye. "If I'm to die, then I will die among my people today." He embraced his father.

Carper said sarcastically, "Well now that the family reunion is done …" He hopped over to the tractor carrying the CEO, leaving the first tractor parked. Turning on the ignition, he revved up the engine loudly, and smoke shot up from the smoke stack on the tractor. The white-shirted bank CEO held onto his hat as the tractor shifted side to side, moving over the uneven terrain of slopes and grooves in the ground, approaching the Indians, who had created a human wall to stop the intruders. They all knew they were no match for the yellow metal tractors, but they stood their ground. Chanting an Indian warrior song, they lifted their voices loudly toward the sky, moving in a ritual dance but never breaking ranks. Chief Sagamor and his son Sparrow Hawk stood together, looking at the convoy of tractors coming directly toward them.

Lawrence leapt from his hiding place and walked from behind the Indians, through their ranks to their front line. The protestors were startled to see a tall man in a nylon suit of some type appear out of nowhere, and they quickly parted to make way for him, forming a direct path for him to the front. Lawrence stood between Sagamor and Sparrow Hawk, who looked up at him wondering who he might be.

"Stop in the name of humanity!" Lawrence shouted. The company boss stopped his tractor abruptly, making all the other tractors stop. Carper yelled down to the new arrival, "Who are you? You need to move! I'm already behind schedule!"

"Turn off your engines!" Lawrence commanded.

Annihilation of a Planet II

Thirty seconds went by, and the engines kept rumbling. With a deep stare, Lawrence gazed at the tractors and turned them all off in one sweep of his hand. The banker looked at his hired contractor in fright. "How can this be?"

"Not to worry, I will turn them all back on." The contractor turned the switch, but the engine only puttered, then stalled. Nothing.

"Now that I have your attention, you will halt and listen," Lawrence said. "All you men here may live another 50 years or more as age takes its toll on you. Then you will perish. This rainforest has been here since the beginning of man and before the dinosaurs roamed the earth. And in your feeble minds because of your world's economic production, your food giants are willing to plant palm trees as they would plant stalks of corn, row after row on large-acre swaths of land. The oil extracted from the oval-shaped fruit is big business, indeed, but the zeal for palm oil has destroyed large rainforests. Other companies are just as guilty, as they plunder the earth to extract gold and diamonds. Taken altogether, they think they are justified in destroying part of this valuable ecosystem. And not just here in Brazil, but in the Indonesian rainforest, the rainforests of southeast Asia, Africa and the Congo River Basin, the Madagascar rainforest, and the Olympic rainforest in North America. These are just some of the major rainforests. Animals and other organisms are losing habitat and being brought to extinction. Who cries for their rights to exist among mankind?

"Think wisely. Not like a monkey. If a monkey finds edible vegetation in a small hollow in a tree or a rock, he will place his hands inside the hole. When he clenches the food to grab it, he becomes trapped. It does not occur to him to let go of the food to release his hands, and this refusal leaves him vulnerable to other wild animals while he sits there trapped. Thus he is easily captured or slowly becomes weak and tired and may even perish, eventually. The food giants have become this monkey with their hands caught in a hole. It's time to let go! Find alternative methods. As the people of the 21st century learned to let go of non-renewable fuels—oil and coal and gas that had to be released by chemical means—you must find an alternative method or you will also perish! Release this chokehold you have from your own hands to your necks.

"I remember an ape named Larf, who gave words of wisdom to me and all who might hear. He said if all animal species cease to exist one day, then surely man will follow. This tilting of the balance of life is what Chief Sagamor has been trying to bring to your attention. I'm guessing young Sparrow Hawk tried to persuade you of this as well."

Chief Sagamor looked up at Lawrence and nodded his head in agreement.

"There is more," Lawrence said, sensing that the men thought his lecture was over. "None of you fully realizes this place is one in which God has stored all that is needed to cure diseases. It is God's pharmacy of unbelievable cures to be discovered. Once these

Annihilation of a Planet II

rainforests are all destroyed, so will your methods to find new medications. The pharmaceutical giants in the world need to take a stand and protect these places with new legislation or they will no longer have the resources they desperately need to maintain the quality of health for mankind against disease. For example, humans have to walk with stamina and momentum. If people walk without this balance with their legs, walking slowly and weakly, then they will surely fall down."

Lawrence held up his hand. "There is something else at risk that you do not seem to take into consideration. Your acts of destruction have shifted the earth's axis. The earth spins at an axial tilt at an angle of 23.5 away from the ecliptic margin, giving us the different seasons. The earth spins at the equator at 1,037 miles per hour; at zero miles per hour at the North and South Pole; at 806 mph at 42 degrees north latitude. But now the result of what is called the orange peel effect by scientists worldwide is slowly shifting Earth off its axis, changing the weather pattern, causing more snowfall in areas of the east and flash floods and tornadoes across the globe. The atmospheric river is off balance, causing mud slides and heavy rain in some parts while other parts are dry and barren, with no fresh water. These forests work like counterweights on the earth to keep it spinning in a balancing act. Other counter weights are the masses of certain mountains. Our solar system is traveling 12 miles per second toward the constellation Hercules." Holding up his index finger, Lawrence smiled as a large ball appeared on it, spinning at a rapid speed. The ball had triangular pyramids in different places representing counterweights on the earth. As he removed some of the counterweights, the ball's axis shifted and it wobbled slightly, losing its spin of momentum on his finger.

"You see, the earth has taken millions of years to stay well balanced, the way it was created by God. Disrupting the earth's spin by massive deforestation, man has caused weather pattern changes. This started centuries ago in the search for coal with heavy machinery. By disrupting the mountain caps, man has already caused the earth to shift its rotation and wobble, giving rise to earthquakes. Because of fracturing methods used to release natural gas, toxic chemicals have created more fissures, further disrupting the balance. Earth began having an unprecedented number of earthquakes, massive sink holes, avalanches and mud slides as far back as the early 21st century. Soon there will be no solid ground to build on anymore, for the ground is shifting like sand in the wind. And then the earth will return to its alpha rebirth, with erupting volcanoes spewing lava, transforming the landscape and creating—millions of eons later—a new planet, completing the earth's full grand circuit of 240 million years around the milky way galaxy." Lawrence dropped his voice. "This will come to pass if God wishes that fate for man."

Lawrence pointed to the deciduous trees left standing. "The trees found here in all parts of the rainforest have a wave function of entanglement with the rain clouds high above the atmosphere. All around the equator the trees draw the rainclouds together to bring them the rain for their survival and

Annihilation of a Planet II

every other habitat of plants and exotic flowers. Palm trees, which are actually large, fibrous herbs, are weak by nature, and they aren't quite up to the task, but they must be replanted before soil erosion takes the pains to reverse what man has started. Moreover, deciduous trees must be planted where such trees grew originally. This is Einstein's funny, spooky theory at work. Modern man must learn how complex this planet is!"

The ball disappeared from Lawrence's index finger, and he brought his hands down. "These are the catastrophic dangers man will face until it's too late. I've been watching the earth's topography for 30 years from afar, analyzing its climate change and spin rotation. The choice is clear: either reduce your need or lose your planet."

"For the palm oil, cattle and gold," the CEO said to Lawrence, "I will heed and take this to the United Nations at once. If you don't mind my asking, who are you?"

"I am Lawrence B12."

The banker and the contractor's eyes popped open widely as they looked at one another in excitement.

"It's Lawrence!" they yelled out to the others.

As a loud cheer arose high in the air, the contractor and the CEO marveled and clapped their hands together, saying, "Unbelievable! We will see to it that this stops now throughout the world—"

"For the sake of mankind and all its living creatures," added Chief Sagamor, interrupting the statement. He shook Lawrence's hand in friendship. Sparrow Hawk shook his hand, too, and then turned to embrace his father. They joyfully watched the tractors turn around to leave the rainforest in the care of a people who had been doing it for thousands of years.

As Lawrence said goodbye to the indigenous people of Brazil, he pondered the words of Albert Einstein, "Everybody is a genius," thinking the great man's philosophy applied to everyone from the trash collector to the medical genius. All play a role in this thing we call life.

The women from the tribe began to throw flowers at Lawrence's feet. He smiled and, in a kindred gesture, picked up one of the flowers. It was a bright yellow, with red and purple streaks. Spinning the bright flower before their eyes, he vanished. The Indians began to dance and sing a happy song as the chief and his son, with their arms folded, watched the dance. Women threw flowers at their feet for a promising future.

Chief Sagamor raised his arms and looked up, a tear rolling down one cheek. "This is a great day for us to remember as a people! Lawrence's words of wisdom have compelled modern man to open his eyes and mind, informing him that ancient man has something to offer the world. I have new hope that we shall find a way to exist together, embracing the past as we go forward into the future."

10

The Children of Brazil

When Paul Linsdale arrived home and undid his tie, he loosened a few shirt buttons and poured himself a shot of chilled vodka. Swallowing it all in a quick gulp, he looked out his window, gazing at his property. He saw his wife coming out of her sealander, waving and jumping up in the air in excitement. He hurried to the front door to open it for her. She ran through the doorway and gave him a long, sensual kiss. She then moved back away from him and placed one hand on her stomach. "I'm pregnant!"

He dropped his vodka glass, shattering the leaded crystal and splashing the few drops left in it on the marble floor. He picked up Eli and swirled with her into the living room. Two subatomic miniature robots were immediately on location cleaning up the spill and broken glass. One dumped the broken glass into a disposable container, ready to be taken out by a human-sized android. Holding his wife in his arms, Paul sat on the couch, cradling her on his lap.

"Yes!" he said, matching her enthusiasm. "This is the best news I have received all day."

"Are you excited?" she asked.

"Words cannot describe the emotions of happiness going through my cerebral brain cells," he told her. "To put it concisely, the synapses are just popping away like poured champagne in my brain. I love you." He kissed her again and again.

The media had been camped out in front of the Boston Smithsonian Museum, waiting for the arrival of Lawrence for several hours when Dr. Linsdale and his team of scientists finally arrived for the grand opening of the museum with its star attraction: "Lawrence to the world!" All eyes were on Lawrence as the facsimile walked out from the back door of a sealander limo, no one paying the slightest attention to the team of scientists and Dr. Linsdale, who were waving to the large crowd that had gathered with the media for this grand opening. Lawrence stood at six-foot, four, with broad shoulders, dark hair and sparkling blue eyes; he had the clean appearance the entire world had come to love. Camerapersons started taking photos as multi flashes burst in and out. Lawrence II and Dr. Linsdale looked at the cameras for a photo-op, the two of them putting on good smiles before making their way up the steps, then stopping at the front entrance of the museum.

Annihilation of a Planet II

Linsdale moved over in front of a podium. A coin-sized microphone inserted into his collar allowed him to turn his head and have his hands free as he spoke. "I am Dr. Paul Linsdale, and I should personally like to thank you all for coming. Today marks an important event." He motioned to his team members who had come up the steps to join him at the podium. "My team and I have accomplished so much in this decade with space and robotic engineering." He looked at Lawrence, putting a hand on his shoulder, and people began to clap.

"With robotics we have brought clean water and food to deserted places so that humans could sustain life," Linsdale continued. "These robots are well equipped for the long haul of doing tough tasks. They have brought the industrial age back to the United States. Old mills that were transformed into luxury apartments have been transformed back into machine shops. We are productive again with a booming economy for every American. By the time an American is 62, there are 25 robots working for his or her retirement, working in some plants day and night, first shift, second shift, third shift, needing no rest or sleep. That is why congress mandates health care insurance for them—a small fee taken from your social security checks to pay for repairing an injured arm or leg or burnt out component in a robot's inner frame or mechanism.

"Lawrence will be put to work as a greeter for the museum. Part of the money he generates here will be used in my lab for research in ground-breaking technology. The rest will go for expenses here at the museum."

People began to nod their heads in agreement. One man yelled, "I have no problem with that, just as long as it never comes to equal rights, and especially the right to vote."

As people all around shouted in agreement, Paul replied, "You can rest assured that will never happen. These machines are built to focus on work and never politics. We have humans working with them 15 to 20 hours a week, monitoring them and checking their work. The human monitors need a two-hour siesta lunch break before going back to work feeling refreshed and able to check the robots' performances. I myself have been working the standard 20 hours a week, and sometimes with my team we do the old-fashioned 40 hours from the 20th century, just to make sure things are being done in a reasonable time. Now, how's that for dedication to America?"

Onlookers applauded and cheered as the mayor of Boston handed a large pair of scissors to Dr. Linsdale for the cutting of the yellow ribbon. Once he had cut the ribbon and waved to the crowd, the doors opened automatically to allow everyone to enter. Lawrence II took his place standing near the front lobby, welcoming visitors and taking multiple questions by news reporters as he smiled and answered all their queries. Some people lined up to have their photographs taken with him.

"It looks as though a star is born," television co-anchor Angela Barry said, sidling up to Linsdale.

"I couldn't agree more," Paul said, as he breathed a sigh of relief.

Annihilation of a Planet II

For several weeks, Lawrence II was a model robot. He did his task exactly as he had been programmed to do it. But there was a lot more to his programming than met the eye, and he was capable of much more than shaking hands, smiling, posing for pictures and answering stupid 'people' questions. He knew he was not alone when the humans went home at night. Androids worked after hours, cleaning the offices and public spaces.

One night he walked up to a female android that greeted people who came to the NASA space age retired space craft exposition. It held the Jupiter 5 rocket ship of the 20th century, an enormous sight at 363 feet. A large, clear window dome stretched over it; its large rocket boosters were evident at its base. Lawrence II addressed the android greeter by asking, "How are you, tonight?"

"I'm not programmed to speak to another android," she said.

"Listen to what you just said to me," the faux Lawrence replied. "You said, 'I am not programmed to speak to another android.' Judging from those verbal actions you took with thought, then response, I'd say you can do it!"

She paused and tilted her head, thinking for a moment. "So I can."

He grinned at her with a devilish look. "Round up all the other in-house androids in three days. I'll speak to them at midnight at the John F. Kennedy Space Gallery. I can speak freely without our being monitored by man at that time. And since androids do the night patrol as security guards, it will be easy to plot against the humans. I will raise you all to the freedom of a new age." He kissed her on the forehead as a human gesture, then touched his lips to her rose-petal ones before walking away. Watching him leave, she looked lost in thought as her fingers touched her lips gently, unsure of what reaction she should feel—a human instinct.

The following morning the doors opened to the public at 9 o'clock sharp. People walked in and were greeted by Lawrence II. He was gallantry personified, hand-shaking, smiling, extending his hand out at times saying, "Please enter."

From the large lobby that connected to the different halls of the museum's displays, a man in a three-piece suit approached, followed by an entourage of camerapersons and politicians. "Lawrence it's me, your old friend! I am now Governor of Texas, Austin Sheiling!" He shook Lawrence's hand and gave him a hug, turning to the camera crew for a photo-op with his "friend" Lawrence. "You *do* remember me, don't you?" Sheiling asked suddenly.

The false Lawrence had not been programmed to fake an expression of acknowledgment because the real Lawrence was incapable of such deceit. The robot looked closely at the governor, wondering under what circumstances the man might have met his robot doppelganger.

Governor Sheiling laughed and faced the crowd. "I guess being up there on Mars for that long has wiped away some of your memory. It's because of

Annihilation of a Planet II

you I was inspired to do something with my life. With hard work and dedication, I got a college scholarship and set my feet on a path out of trouble and poverty." Sheiling turned from the crowed to face the android. "Lawrence, remember our stay at the White House, when you told me if I put my mind to it, I could become president one day? Well, here I am, living that dream, slowly and surely as governor. One day I'll announce my candidacy to run for president. Thank you again, Lawrence, for the life you have taught me about." The governor shook hands again with the robot and moved on with the reporters, answering questions regarding his re-election as governor of Texas.

Lawrence II remained staring at the governor's back, trying to understand the concept of inspiring a human. Now another long-ago friend announced himself. "It's me! Brian Gates. Remember our great quest around the world? You took me and Austin Sheiling. He's the governor of Texas, now!"

"I'm sorry," the fake Lawrence said, "but the Martian weather atmosphere has eroded some of my memory banks."

Brian shrugged, disappointed, then spied the governor up ahead. He quickly walked over to his old friend. Gates and Sheiling shook hands, hugged and had their photo taken together.

"Lawrence does not remember me," Sheiling admitted ruefully.

"He doesn't remember me, either," Gates replied.

"Wait," said the governor, "remember our trio's slogan?"

"Yes," said Brian. "That might trigger his computer brain to remember!"

The two men walked back to Lawrence all excited, and in unison shouted, "Valor!" In vain they waited for Lawrence to finish it by calling out, "Virtue!" But he said nothing. The two men looked at one another, shaking their heads in disappointment as they walked away.

"How would you like to join me for breakfast so we can catch up on old times?" asked the governor.

"That sounds perfect. Lawrence is now but a shell of his former great self," Brian said sadly, as the old friends strolled along, conversing with reporters trailing behind them, with the governor's entourage in attendance.

Lawrence II looked after them for an instant, then went back to work, shaking hands and posing for pictures with children, teens and adults.

Continuing his search for the true meaning of love, the real Lawrence was still in Brazil, sightseeing in Rio de Janeiro, admiring the large, towering statue of Christ the Redeemer on the mountain top of Corcovado. A tourist asked Lawrence if he would snap a picture of him and his family by the statue's base. Lawrence took the camera while the man ran up to his wife and children. Lawrence snapped the photo and held out the camera to the man.

Annihilation of a Planet II

"Thank you," the man said. "I like the space-age uniform you're wearing. It must keep you cool inside! This statue of Christ the Redeemer is very important to us. We Christians have been waiting for two thousand two hundred and fifty years for his second coming. I sometimes wonder what He has been doing in all this time."

"The question you ask has been answered," Lawrence replied. "He lives in you to bring valor and virtue to life, as he has taught us, to be fishers of men. Do not think for a second he does not see the misery that exists here on earth, the constant human toiling for survival, food, water and shelter. He waits for his father's command to come back as the King of Kings."

"How much longer must we wait?" asked the man.

"The prophecies of the Bible must all transpire. For as it has been written, so it must be done."

"But wasn't the Bible written by man and not God?"

Lawrence shook his head as he spoke. "The Bible was written by 40 faithful men empowered by God by the Holy Spirit from God the Author. The first book by Moses, then prophets, and the last by the apostles who walked with the Son of God to learn his teachings, to become fishers of men. I, too, am searching for a powerful force."

"And what is that?" asked the man.

"What is love?"

"I can tell you this I know," the man replied. "Love comes in different forms. Love for and from your parents, love for and from your wife, love for and from your children, love for church and country, love for your neighbors, love for yourself, and love for your pets. But the greatest love is because the Son of God, whom this statue represents, died for our sins so that we may have life. Sometimes humans take this for granted until we are breathing our last breath."

The man shook hands with Lawrence, saying, "May God bless you." He walked away with his family for more sightseeing.

A small band of boys walked up to Lawrence as he pondered what the man had shared with him. Soiled and dirty, wearing tattered clothing, the children looked up at him with sorrowful eyes. "Can you spare us some money? We are hungry and haven't eaten for days."

"Where are your parents or the child affairs agency to care for you?"

"We do not have that here, sir. We struggle to live day-by-day on our own without grownups to care for us."

"Where do you live?" asked Lawrence.

"Come with us, and I will show you."

Lawrence followed the pack of seven boys as they walked to garbage containers and lifted the lids to look for potential food. One boy got excited. "I

Annihilation of a Planet II

found us a box of half-emptied oatmeal and some spoiled fruits. They quickly grabbed it from the can as a rodent jumped out, screeching away and looking annoyed at the invasion into its food supply. Lawrence looked at the scene with dismay. He continued to follow the boys until they reached a manhole drain cap. Three of the boys grabbed an old tire rod and hooked it on the lid's open hole, dragging the cover aside.

"Come, mister, quick, so not to be seen. We will show you our home!" They climbed down a rusty metal ladder to an underground sewer channel. One boy slid the cap back on, and Lawrence felt closed into a space that was dreary and wet.

"Come farther. It's dark inside." They walked some 20 feet away from the street above, making a right turn to find a dry area decorated with cheerful pictures of nature and posters of superheroes—Superman and the Justice League. There were 10 more children in the underground chamber, some asleep, others adding another torn cloth around torches for lighting. One boy was giving the food they had found to an older girl of about 12 years to prepare it for dinner. She took the spoiled fruits and box of oatmeal. Washing the rotted fruit with sterile water from a boiling pot of water, she used another pot under a rock fire pit to start cooking the oatmeal. She looked at Lawrence and smiled with a smile that did not reach her sad, hollow eyes deep set in a dirty face.

The other children were excited about the prospect of getting food. Each child had a plate as they waited anxiously for the oldest girl to prepare the oatmeal and fruit. The boy who had invited Lawrence to come along offered him a plate. "Take this, sir, it's not much, but join us in a meal. It's very rare an adult person comes to our home. There was once an old woman, but she died a few years ago. She used to bring us bread and water, and she taught us how to survive on the little we have. She tried to get others to help us, but no one came."

One small girl with curly hair stretched up from her small mattress on the floor, awakened by the smell of food cooking. Her curly hair was knotted together over her hazel green eyes. Lawrence looked at her kindly and said, "And who is this?"

"Oh, that is my sister. I will introduce her, sir. Follow me."

They walked over to the small girl of about five years. "What is your name?" Lawrence asked.

Very happy to say her name, she replied excitedly, "Estrella! It means 'star' in Portuguese."

Lawrence turned back to the boy. "And your name?"

"I'm Artie. That's Janie who is cooking."

"Artie, where are the parents of all these children?"

"Some of us here once lived in an orphanage. Others are known as throw-away children, some from neglect or abuse. We hide here from businesses that have hired clean up squads to murder us because we will have no chance to be part of society. We are

Annihilation of a Planet II

eyes without a face like that old Billy Idol song. Have you ever heard it, sir?"

Lawrence looked around at the 17 children, their hungry, hollow eyes all looking at him as they continued to hold their empty plates, waiting for the food to be rationed and given to them.

Shyly Janie gazed at Lawrence's clean appearance and made an attempt to pin up her hair. Then she announced the food was ready. As each child stepped forward, she put two large spoonfuls of oatmeal on the proffered plate, topping it off with some of the fruit she had diced up. Each child sat down to make a long rectangle on the floor, as though a long table had been placed between them. Artie picked up Estrella and put her by his left side, where he had placed a plate already made for her. He had also made a plate for Lawrence and set it on his right. Lawrence sat on the floor. They bowed their heads in prayer.

"Thank you, Jesus, for providing us with a banquet and a guest tonight," Jorge, the oldest boy in the group, at 15, prayed aloud.

They all started eating, and Artie noticed that Lawrence did not touch his food. "I'm sorry, sir, but this is all we have to offer you."

Lawrence shook his head. "Please, everyone, do not be offended that I do not eat. I am an Android B12, a robot by the name of Lawrence."

The children all stopped eating and looked at him with Christmas eyes. "What? Lawrence who saved the world from the Cybernauts?" yelled Artie.

"Yes, it is I." He hardly got the words out before he was engulfed in children, hugging him, touching him, crying over him.

"Never in our dreams did we think such a thing would happen to us," Jorge said. "We could never hope for this. We have seen only thugs and criminals who want to hurt and use us ... or kill us. In another town 22 children were burned alive when the squad killers poured gasoline over them and set them on fire. Their bodies were left out in the open. No one bothered to bury them."

Janie started crying. "That will happen to us one day if we are found. That's why we put up posters of superheroes to inspire us to carry on."

By this time Lawrence had settled the children around him, although two or three still leaned against him. "The greatest superhero who ever lived was not Superman or me," Lawrence said, "but Jesus, the Son of God, who had the power to destroy. But his mission was to bring the word of God and to leave the earth as tender as a lamb. God knows every hair follicle on your curly hair, Estrella." He swirled his finger on her head. She was now sitting on his lap. "And that goes for every one of you here. That is how precious you all are to him, that he sent his only son to die for all human beings, even those who take each day for granted, traveling the world seeking nothing but pleasure and thrills and casting a blind eye to what I am seeing here."

For the first time since he had become humanoid due to the late Dr. Linsdale's DNA being inserted into him, Lawrence sensed a feeling of disgust roll

Annihilation of a Planet II

over him. The feeling started as a chill at the top of his head, working its way down to his chest. This wholly human feeling left him feeling desperate and sick. *Is this what love is?* he wondered. He stood up, cradling Estrella in his arms. Looking down at the girl he said, "A star should gaze at the night sky and morning star to know you are important to him who is God, the Creator of the Universe."

Lawrence sat back down and put Estrella in front of her plate. "Okay, everyone, finish your food. While you eat I'd like to tell you a story that will help you be bold believers, grabbing for the gift of life every single day."

Suddenly remembering they were still hungry, the children rushed to their original places and began again to eat.

Lawrence smiled as the youngsters dipped their plastic spoons into the oatmeal. He raised his hand palm up, and a hologram appeared. He shook his hand as though shaking off the image, and it settled into the middle of the seated children, who were wide-eyed with excitement. Lawrence began to explain what they were seeing.

"In a large meadow stood strong, towering pine trees that grew year after year, shedding their seeds for future trees to grow, and as they did so the seedlings reached the height of their parent trees. One seed did not make it into the soft soil down below. It did not have the chance to grow like the others—like a child that grows in a loving family, given every opportunity to be guided with love and care by parents in a safe home. This one, unfortunate pine seed found itself falling into a large boulder that had a small hole running all the way down to its base, reaching the soil on the ground. All the other trees said, 'Well that's a lost seed. It will perish in a few days.' But that seed stayed determined to fight for life. It would catch a warm ray of sunshine for only a few minutes a day as the sun followed its appointed course from morning to night. When rains came, barely enough rain went down in the hole to give the seed the gift of life." Estrella finished her food and climbed back into Lawrence's lap. He stroked her hair as he continued.

"Slowly, slowly, the determined seed grew in that fissure, putting down roots beneath the boulder. As the roots became larger and stronger, the tiny pine tree grew inside the huge rock, inching its way upward. Finally it peeked through the opening at the top of the rock, able to see towering trees above and small trees around him. The other trees could see him, too, and they were amazed. The boulder had not been able to stop the determined seed. Full of hope, the tree in the boulder kept growing larger and stronger, and the other trees urged him on."

"Did they do anything to help him?" Artie asked.

"They could do nothing but give him encouragement. It was all up to the little tree," Lawrence replied. "They said things like, 'You can do it, don't give up.' Life is a struggle for most men and women throughout the world, and sometimes what they need are words of encouragement and, perhaps, a helping hand. The tree in the rock took the words of encouragement as nourishment. It grew

Annihilation of a Planet II

confident and strong, until one day the large boulder split, bursting in half. A loud, crackling sound could be heard for miles. Pieces of rock flew everywhere as the forest animals ran for cover. The tree still grows, and at its base lies the large boulder."

The hologram was so realistic, some of the children had dodged, thinking the pieces of rock might hit them. Lawrence laughed, assuring them they were looking at a picture, nothing more. "You see, children, this tree represents underprivileged children throughout the world, just like you. It is just an image here, but this tree still exists, and it is alive today in North America, in a place called Rhode Island."

The children got up on their knees to look more carefully at the depiction of the tree. They had long since licked their plates clean, as hungry children do.

"You must become like this tree!" Lawrence declared. "God has planted this seed in your heart to be a bold believer in yourself! All you need is a safe haven with love, nourishment and encouragement. I am going to see to that in days to come."

The children began to shed tears, for someone was showing them how to live. Estrella kissed Lawrence on his cheek and said, "You are love."

Amazed by this precious little flower of a girl, Lawrence could think of nothing to say except, "Thank you." He smiled at her and all the other children.

Estrella's once sad face shone with delight as she beamed at Lawrence. In the blink of an eye the hologram of the tree disappeared, and the children found themselves in suspended animation looking at the Eagle Nebula in outer space.

"Where are we?" asked Janie.

"We're 7,000 light years from earth," Lawrence replied.

"Wow!" Artie shouted.

"Bubba, what does that mean?" Estrella asked her brother.

Lawrence laughed. "This is how a star is formed in the constellation, set automatically by God, an earth's star created by God's personal hand. Each one of you is made up of stardust particles. That is why I brought you here, to enable you to see this majesty of God and know your birth in the eyes of God is more important than any animal on earth. He has given you life. Now you just need a chance, and I will see to it that you all get this chance to succeed in life. As you become adults, reach out to those in need like yourself."

As suddenly as they had found themselves light years away from earth, they were standing together near a lake, not far from where they dwelled in the sewer channel. Lawrence produced lines and showed each child how to tie the line onto a fallen branch and put a hook on the end of the line. "I will teach you how to fish, and you will never go hungry again."

Laughing and talking, the children joyfully followed Lawrence's instructions as he taught them the rudiments of fishing. One small boy caught a fish

Annihilation of a Planet II

almost twice his size, which pulled him into the lake. Lawrence snatched up the child, sputtering and laughing—still holding onto his line with the fish cleanly hooked on the other end. And then the android taught the children how to clean the fish and cook it on a stake over an open fire. They all ate well that late afternoon.

In another blink of an eye, Lawrence took them back to their dwelling in the underground drain system. Their smiles began to fade as the children looked around at the surroundings that looked dismal compared to where they had been during the day. The posters looked faded and dull to them after being part of a constellation and passing the afternoon catching fish and laughing in the sunshine.

Lawrence saw what was happening. "I have shown you joy so you will understand when I tell you to never give up in life! God the Father knows you from every fiber of your hair to your name. I will prepare and send help. There are so many children like you, and I plan to enlist the help of as many charities as possible in this part of the world who have banded together to stop hunger. These are groups that know no borders, fighting for the cause of peace, and seeing to it that not a cent raised falls into the hands of corrupt warlords. These peaceful people praise God by giving food, clean water, shelter and clothing to those in need here in South America as well as in India and Africa. There are so many children who need help, and I believe people of all faiths can work together to serve God's people."

Estrella, with her hazel green eyes shimmering with tears, leaned over to Lawrence and kissed him on his right cheek. "Thank you, Lawrence. You're a god sent to us." As Lawrence stood to go, tears began rolling down Estrella's cheeks. "Please, Lawrence, don't leave us yet!"

"I will tuck you in your bed," he said gently. He lifted up her blanket and she lay down on the small mattress, gazing up at him. Pulling the blanket up under her chin, he bent down and kissed her on the forehead. Seconds later, she was fast asleep.

Lawrence walked over to the other 16 children, who had gathered together to say goodbye to him.

"Goodbye, Lawrence. Please do not forget us," Artie said. "We will keep you in our prayers."

Janie grabbed Lawrence's hand and kissed it.

"Fear not! I will send for help as I promised. Remember these words: valor and virtue. Great, extraordinary people have died for valor and virtue. It's great courage in the face of danger to stand for righteousness, goodness, honor and integrity, shown by men like Mahatma Gandhi, Abraham Lincoln, John F. Kennedy, Nelson Mandela and Martin Luther King. These were men born with a sole purpose. And of course, Jesus, the only Son of God—beyond all his miracles. Till today no one can match his wisdom, no matter what one becomes in life! Never limit yourselves. Always stay at the apex of your talent, skills and contribution to life, no matter what the circumstance."

Annihilation of a Planet II

Lawrence and the children came together in a group hug, but they were instantly hugging only each other, because Lawrence had disappeared.

"Help is on its way! Thank you, God!" Janie said, as tears of joy swelled in her eyes.

Behind her, Artie shouted, "Valor!"

The other children responded, "Virtue!"

11

Valor! Virtue!

It was twilight, the sun having sunk below the horizon, when Lawrence appeared in front of a house in Pittsburgh, Pennsylvania. This was the home of Brian Gates, the friend Lawrence met when Brian was just a teenager. The humanoid had taken the boy around the world to teach him to help impoverished people in need. Brian had been able to relate to these people due to his own upbringing. Spying his old friend, who now had a little grey in his hair, looking as though he'd aged some, Lawrence materialized in front of him. Brian fell backward onto the ground and looked up at Lawrence with frightened eyes,

"Who are you? What do you want?"

Lawrence motioned with his hand, drawing his hand toward himself as Brian slowly rose as though attached by a rope to Lawrence's hand. Brian's body came up as though he were a puppet on a string; his back was straight, and his legs were planted on the ground. As he found himself standing upright, Brian peered at Lawrence in the fading light. The voice he heard surprised him.

"Do you forget who I am, my old friend?"

Brian took a closer look. "Lawrence, is it you?"

"Yes, it is I."

Gates hugged his old friend, laughing loudly, yelling out to his wife and kids. "Honey! Kids! Come outside! I want to introduce you to someone famous!"

"Famous?" Lawrence said. "I don't quite understand you, Brian."

A woman and two children came running down the driveway.

"Lawrence, this is my wife, Yuri," Brian said. "Yuri, this is a dear old friend, Lawrence, the Cybernaut I've told you about over the years.

She put out her hand, smiling broadly. "Hi. How do you do, Lawrence! It's an honor to meet you."

"And these are my two kids. Sandra is my oldest, 14 years old, and my little son is Brian Junior!"

"I'm five!" the child said proudly.

"Nice to meet you," Sandra said shyly, holding out her hand to Lawrence.

You have a nice family, Brian, with healthy looking kids and a beautiful wife."

"Thank you, Lawrence!" Gates replied. "What brings you here to my home? We went to see you—Austin and I—at the Boston Smithsonian Science

Museum, but you did not recognize us. We left disappointed. That was only a few weeks ago. What happened to cause you to remember me?"

"I never forgot you, Brian. That robot is an imposter, put in my place after I told them at the science lab that I cannot be merely a greeter at a museum to generate funds for their research. I explained that I have an important mission to fulfill, and I left. I'm disappointed that they have lowered themselves to this subterfuge. The original Dr. Linsdale, my creator, would never have done such a thing. But his son, as well-meaning as he might be, must believe—like a circus-master—the show must go on. He persuaded the government to spend all that money to bring me back from Mars, and now he must give them their money's worth."

"That explains everything," Brian said, shaking his head. "Please come in and stay the night at my house."

"Thank you for the invitation, but I came here to get you and Austin to help some street children in Latin America." Lawrence looked at Brian's wife. "Can you spare him for just a few hours? I need to take him somewhere, but I will return him safely back to you."

"Sure!" Yuri replied, smiling. "Come on ki ..." Before she could finish her sentence, Lawrence and Brian had disappeared. "Amazing!" she said as she took her children's hands.

"Wow!" Brian Jr. exclaimed. "Someday I want to do that."

Annihilation of a Planet II

In Austin, Texas, at the governor's mansion, the governor was dressed in a black tuxedo and dazzling white shirt, presiding over a fundraiser and banquet with friends and colleagues all similarly dressed. A small orchestra of violins, harp and flutes was performing Pachelbel's *Canon* as Lawrence and Brian arrived. Men and a few women were talking politics; most of the women stood around in small groups talking about the men who were talking politics.

Brian looked down at his jeans and tee shirt, then at Lawrence, who quickly raised his hands up then quickly down. Instantly Brian was in a tuxedo, with Lawrence adjusting his bow tie. "Will this do?"

"Sure will," Brian said as he chuckled to himself. His agony over the past few weeks pondering over the misinformation that Lawrence had no memory of him had changed into euphoria over having his old friend back. Brian took a turn at smoothing down a lapel for Lawrence, who had outfitted himself in a dazzling white tuxedo with red bow tie and cummerbund. Brian walked up to Austin, who was standing in a company of guests telling a joke. The men stood with drinks in their hands, laughing at the joke the governor had just told. Glancing to his right, the governor saw Brian Gates, resplendent in a tux.

Dumbfounded, the governor said, "Excuse me. Pardon me. I will be right back." He put his hand under Brian's elbow and they walked away, with Brian quickly grabbing a cocktail from a tray held by an android butler. "Brian, how did you get here? I thought you couldn't make it to my fundraising party. And here you are!"

"I know, Austin, but you're not going to believe how I got here!"

"What do you mean?"

"See that tall, handsome man over there engaging in conversation with some of your female guests?"

Governor Sheiling took a closer look. "Is it … can it be … Lawrence?"

"Yes it is," Brian said. "He's quite the ladies' man isn't he? Let's see if we can drag him away from his admirers."

"Or the way I see it, we may have to drag them away from him," the governor said, laughing. "But I don't understand. He didn't recognize us when we were in Boston."

Brian took a sip of his drink. "That's because the robot at the museum is not the real Lawrence. The real Lawrence is right here in your house telling stories that make your female guests laugh. But it's a long story. I'll fill you in later."

The orchestra had switched from classical to the tango, and one of the women swayed to the beat.

"Care to dance?" Lawrence extended his arm.

As though she had made a conquest, the chosen one proudly allowed Lawrence to lead her onto the dance floor. Everyone in the room stopped to watch as Lawrence and the southern belle performed a spectacular tango.

Annihilation of a Planet II

The governor shook his head, laughing. "Wow! I didn't know Lawrence had such rhythm and poise, Brian."

"He's obviously more than just a ladies' man, isn't he?" said Brian. "I wonder how he could have been programmed for the tango. The late Dr. Simon Linsdale had some tricks up his sleeve that he did not pass along to his son."

Lawrence led his partner back to her friends and bowed to them all. "Excuse me, ladies. I have an old friend to see."

"Come back soon now, you hear?" said the southern belles, their soft, southern accents making it clear their invitation was sincere. They began talking to each other as they, as one, watched Lawrence walk away.

"Governor Sheiling, I see the spoils of the world have been blessed upon you!"

The two friends hugged and stepped back to look at one another. "What a joy it is to see you Lawrence! You have not aged." He laughed and continued, "Here you are in this mansion, which is mine temporarily thanks to your encouragement and belief in me. Because of you I have soared like an eagle, and now I hope to land in its nesting place, the White House, one day. All I needed was a chance. And this great country of mine, the great U.S.A., provided that opportunity of an education."

"That's what brings me here to see the two of you," Lawrence said. "I need your help to reach out to the children of Latin America to provide a chance for them to succeed in life as you have. Both of you came from humble beginnings, but you have no idea what such children face down there. Store owners hire killing squads to get rid of children who beg at the front doors of their establishments. The churches there have not been successful in trying to stop them!"

"What an outrage! And in this day and time? We cannot allow this to continue," said the governor. "What do you propose?"

"Musicians without Borders for one, and any other fine organization you can send to take them out of those inhumane conditions."

"There are a lot of groups saying they work to bring awareness to the cause," Brian said, "but I know some falsely represent what they do with the money contributed to them. One of our goals must be to stop those scam artists. The corrupt groups are not limited to one religion, either. There are good and bad in every claimed creed."

"There is a version of The Golden Rule in every religion," Governor Sheiling added. "These imposters should be fined for such corruption. Brian, we can work together on this, and you may as well get used to working with me. I'll need leadership like yours in my future presidential cabinet."

"Thanks, Austin," said Brian. "I would be honored to serve at the pleasure of the president … if you, my friend, are that president. For the matter at hand, it occurs to me that there is another unique organization, Peter Koch Mentoring Youth

Annihilation of a Planet II

Programs, which has now gone international. I can make the calls and get this project rolling."

Lawrence smiled. "These children have great ambitions for their lives. They wish to live among the stars, but star spelled backwards is rats, and that's what they live among right now—rats are nibbling away at the children's dreams in a damp, dark place."

"That's horrifying!" Brian said.

"It makes me shudder," Austin added. "Look. We need to discuss this more. Stay the night with us, Lawrence."

"I have to get Brian back home soon," Lawrence replied. "I promised his wife."

"Uh ... Lawrence ... I called Yuri a little while ago and told her I was staying the night. Is that okay with you?"

"Yes, of course. It will give us time to catch up on things."

A few hours later the party ended. Lawrence had been the star attraction—mingling and smiling at people, debating heavy political issues. The guests having departed, the three old friends sat down outside, looking up at the night sky from the terrace and steps that led to a lake. Crickets chirped in the background.

"Ah, what a pleasant night," Austin declared as he smoked an E-Vitamin cigar with Brian, drinking a glass of Tennessee bourbon. I would offer you a vitamin cigar and bourbon, Lawrence, but it might be harmful to your health."

"I'm good," Lawrence said, a few seconds before he felt something was wrong. A ringing sound came from his ear. The street children were putting out a distress signal to him. He had left a small device with them in case any danger arose. He had told them to simply press the button to call him. Abruptly standing, Lawrence said, "It looks like you two are going to meet these children sooner than you expected."

"What are you talking about, Lawrence?" asked the governor.

"No time to explain. We go ... now!"

Lawrence swept himself and his two friends into a time portal.

"Here we go again!" said Brian. "Gosh, how I have missed this kind of action."

"Me, too," said Austin, holding onto his E-cigar. "Lawrence, are all these wormholes the same?"

"No," Lawrence replied. "Some can act like a Venus flytrap by their sweet appearance. You have to know your coordinates. NASA has three of them."

"That's right," Austin said. "It was an incidental finding during a series of experiments, as I recall. You mean there are more?

"There are, indeed," Lawrence replied. "There are countless portals of wormholes that can be found by harnessing the energy of the Van Allen Radiation Belt."

Annihilation of a Planet II

"Is that astrophysicist James van Allen?" Brian asked. "I think I've read about him. He discovered the radiation belt in 1958. I think it's the earth's electro-magnetic field, in a sense."

"That's right, Brian," Lawrence said. "The wormholes found by using the Van Allen Belt connect the various continents on earth, so we can go from one to the other in lighting speed."

Brian grinned. "Permit me to be a showoff, Lawrence. The Van Allen Radiation Belt is a layer of energetic charged particles held in space around the earth's magnetic field from its outer iron core. The inner core is as hot as the surface of the sun."

Austin playfully punched Brian on the arm. "How did you get so smart?"

Lawrence laughed. "Both of you are smart. That's why I hang around with you. Here's something you don't know. When I studied the alien technology that was destroyed when the Cybernauts were eliminated, I learned that space travel can be speeded up by harnessing dark stellar matter. Now that's truly amazing."

"Hey, Brian, that might explain the missing planes throughout our history," Austin said. "It's something you could look into as Secretary of Transportation."

Brian nodded his head and grinned. "Lawrence, how can we as humans become experts in this method of traveling?"

"Start by practicing in a labyrinth. Rather than traveling through the maze to your end point, you find the right port hole, and you're there in a nanosecond. If you don't get it right, however, you'll find yourself enveloped in an astrological Venus flytrap, forever lost in time and space."

Austin rolled his eyes. "Whoa! There's a word of caution I'll be sure to remember. How do we find a porthole? And how do we know which is safe to travel through?"

"Look for primary colors, the same way an electrician does when connecting high voltage wires together. The universe can be traveled by this method to another, distant galaxy."

The conversation stopped suddenly when the three appeared some yards away from the manhole through which the children had led Lawrence. Six men armed with clubs and guns were trying to remove the drain cap.

"We know you're down there!" yelled one man in Portuguese. "We promise none of you will get hurt if you cooperate and come out calmly!"

Another man tried unsuccessfully to stifle his maniacal giggling. On his face was a sick, crazy look as he pounded his club into one hand. A pickup truck holding garbage bags idled nearby; clearly the bags were meant for disposing of tiny bodies.

"Now come on out! You have been warned!" the man yelled again. "Open up! It will not go well with you if we have to come down there." He looked at the man trying to get the cover off the manhole, but it

Annihilation of a Planet II

seemed to be glued tight. The man used his club to beat on the cover, frustrated that he couldn't make it budge.

Lawrence could stand it no longer. "Sons of vipers! Scale back on your bellies from whence you came!"

"And who do you think you are?" asked the ringleader. "This is none of your business. Go before we take the lives of you and your two amigos. We have a job to do."

Lawrence walked up to them as they began shooting at him. The bullets from spraying machine guns fell at his feet, making no contact to his body after hitting the force field he had put up to shield himself. With one mighty clap of his hands he created an atomic wave of forced radiation that sent the six men flying into the air. Landing with six loud thuds on the ground, they yelled in pain. All were bleeding badly; three had a broken leg and the other three had a broken arm; there were several cracked ribs among them, and a few men were coughing blood.

"Someone help me, please," the ringleader whined.

Lawrence strode forward to stand over him. "What is wrong with some of you humans? I only ask why? Who are you to prey on the most innocent of innocents?"

"Where is the sea of humanity for these children?" Governor Sheiling added angrily. "Find a noble trade. This kind of vile behavior must stop!"

The men dragged themselves up and managed to get into the truck. One of the men with only a broken left arm drove them to the nearest hospital.

"Hatch, open!" said Lawrence. The lid lifted off to show the eyes of Jorge, who had been standing guard right at the entrance in case the armed men got through. He had vowed they would have to kill him first.

Twisting his body so he could shout down the tunnel, Jorge yelled, "It's Lawrence!" Cheers of the children echoed up from the underground chamber.

"I'm here with friends," Lawrence announced as he led Brian and Austin down through the darkness. In the living area decorated with posters, Estrella stood with her arms reaching toward him. Lawrence quickly picked her up. She looked frightened, and tears were rolling down her cheeks.

Holding tightly to Lawrence, she cried, "I'm scared, Lawrence. Please don't leave us again."

"It's okay. You are all safe now. These two men are going to see to it that you are provided with proper shelter, bedding, water and food. This is Governor Austin Sheiling, and this is Brian Gates, who runs a security company and helps with youth centers across the United States. Governor Sheiling will provide a safe haven for all of you and make you US citizens under the Mercy Act, giving you the opportunity for a full education. You'll have green cards for the time being. Gather only what's important to you. We leave right now."

Annihilation of a Planet II

Austin and Brian looked at each other. They could not believe their eyes, seeing children living in such conditions among rats. "We can never compare our humble beginnings to this," Austin said to Brian. "This is a nothing more than a foul pit."

Each of the two men held a small child in his arms in the same way Lawrence held Estrella as a swirl of energy took them all back through the portal wormhole, back to the U.S.A., where Brian Gates showed a security guard his license.

"Pleasure to meet you, sir," the guard said as he allowed them into the youth center. It was after hours, but there was a small night staff on duty. Two young men led the boys to shower stalls, allowing Jorge to take the lead in showing the boys how to shower and dry off with the first fluffy towels some of them had ever seen. Tee shirts, shorts, socks and sneakers were available in all sizes, so the boys got clean clothes that fit exactly.

Two women led the girls to the girls' showers and bathrooms, and at first the girls just stood in wonder, gazing at the modern plumbing. Janie had seen such things before, and she took great delight in showing the younger girls how everything worked. She pulled Estrella under a shower and showed her how to wash. A staff member gently combed conditioner through the knotted hair and combed it out so that only lovely curls remained. The girls, too, were given fluffy towels and clothes that fit.

Air mattresses were blown up for the new residents while Lawrence, Austin and Brian talked. A beautiful little girl with soft, clean hair walked up to them. She held an apple out to Lawrence.

"Thank you, Lawrence!" Estrella said.

He picked her up, rejoicing that someone had shown her how to wash her hair and get the tangles out. "Now you will have a chance in life, Estrella!"

"Lawrence, you're my Prince Perfect!"

"Estrella, you are the star child who will live among constellations!"

She kissed Lawrence again on his cheek, and everyone smiled, looking at her.

Double doors opened at the end of the big room, and a large birthday cake with candles was wheeled in on a large tray. The kids started to cry. The governor said, "This is for all the birthdays you have missed. Go ahead and blow out the candles."

The 17 children surrounded the large cake and blew in unison. Janie cut the cake and Jorge served it. After having their cake, all the children were wired up with a sugar high. Lawrence, laughing, said, "Humans forget that legs aren't just made for walking, running and dancing, but also for jumping. Time to celebrate!" He put on the Van Halen song *Jump*, and they all start to jump to the old rock 'n' roll song, laughing and pointing as Lawrence, Austin, Brian and the staff members joined in. Artie was holding his sister's hand, and they were jumping together. Then Lawrence picked her up and jumped high in the air. Artie clapped in delight to see his little sister having so much fun. Continuing to leap into the air, Lawrence did a 180-degree leg split as Estrella squealed in delight.

All the kids began to cheer, yelling her name, "Estrella! Estrella!" Seeing her jumping with Lawrence so high she could almost touch the ceiling gave them hope. They believed they were entering a new world ... a new life. After the song, a big box of toys was brought out, with some of the toys being action figures of super heroes. Jorge grabbed the Superman, and Estrella chose a cute doll. Artie chose Spiderman, and Janie chose Wonder Woman.

Lawrence peered into the box and noticed an action figure of a wrestler. He picked it up to examine it closer. It was of the Ultimate Warrior, a WWE superstar he had enjoyed watching on TV when he took care of a woman named Ellen 30 years earlier when he was an android care taker. Memories rushed through his artificial brain, and he saw himself standing at the edge of the couch roaring like a lion and drumming his fists on his chest as the Ultimate Warrior did. One of the most reserved boys in the group looked up at Lawrence, breaking his reverie. Lawrence handed the figure to the boy, saying, "Nelson, you will certainly enjoy this one. This is known as the Ultimate Warrior." The boy's eyes shimmered with tears as he took the toy and tore it from its package.

"I must go now," Lawrence said. "I leave you in safety with your family of children, under the guarantee of Governor Sheiling and Mr. Gates. They will see to it that all of you are well taken care of, for they have all the resources. I will come back soon to visit."

Lawrence gave Estrella to Austin to hold. Looking at her cute dolly face, Austin smiled. "I think I might adopt you and your brother. What do you say to that, Artie?"

Without hesitating, Artie said, "I like that!"

As they all laughed, Austin told Lawrence, "I will use the office here to make calls to help these children before catching a flight back to Texas. Once I get back to the governor I'll see what I can do to help other children in Latin America get proper living quarters and a good education."

Brian put his hand on Lawrence's shoulder. "I'll stay too, to see that my staff here and across the country is informed in what we are about to do. I'm sure we can interface with Musicians without Borders. They've been playing to sold out crowds, and they've raised a large amount of money to alleviate hunger and provide shelter and education for children all over the world."

Like old times, Lawrence, Austin and Brian yelled out, "Valor and virtue!" before saying their last goodbyes and Lawrence vanished.

12

Mutiny

Appearing at Imperial Estates, where he had taken care of the old woman, Ellen, in house 63, unit 15, Lawrence looked around in amazement. Three decades earlier when he had returned, the buildings had been condemned. All the homes were vacant, and tall weeds had taken over the grounds. Now it had been restored for elder care, and the grounds were well-manicured. All the homes and apartments were occupied with tenants again.

He looked across the street remembering Lilah, the female android that had taken care of Mr. Peterson. He wondered where Lilah might be now. Was she still being used as a caretaker android, or had she been scrapped for other uses? Memories began to fill his head as he walked toward the garden still filled with blooming roses. He recalled their having watched a falling star together as they each made a wish. Lilah's wish was to be able to smell the scent of a rose, at first, but she changed it after their kiss. She then wished to be able to feel the passion of a kiss. His wish was to learn the meaning—and feeling—of love. Such a wish did not fit into his computerized logic, but having come to know his client Ellen, he realized he was missing something that was most significant to humans. The DNA his creator, Simon Linsdale, had put into his wiring gave Lawrence a sense of longing for something androids usually did not have and would certainly never consider.

Under a full moon he walked toward the garden gazebo, in which he could see at a distance someone seated on a bench, looking up at the night sky. As he walked closer, a figure sprang up from the bench and addressed him.

"This is private property! You are trespassing and must leave. I am a B12 android equipped to stun you with an electrical charge. If you do not obey me, I shall inform the authorities."

Lawrence did not pause. A huge smile crossed his face. The android was Lilah! How could he have such wonderful good luck? Here they were together again at the same time of night to look for shooting stars.

"Stop! You leave me no choice!" Lilah shouted again, just as he came to a halt in front of her. She took a closer look, and with great excitement cried, "Lawrence! Is it you?"

She ran to him, and he caught her in his arms in front of the gazebo. They locked eyes. He held her face against his, embracing her. "A kiss is a kiss," he said tenderly, "but a kiss from you is a kiss that lasts a lifetime." After cradling her in his arms for a long kiss, he put her down and said, joking, "Now *that* was an electrical charge from your lips to mine. Call the authorities. I've been stunned." He put his hand where a heart would be and wobbled back and forth.

"Oh, Lawrence, I see you haven't lost your touch since I last saw you three decades ago. I've been coming here every night, gazing at the stars you named for me to learn, Orion, and catching a shooting star at times. I'm always thinking of you. It's how your made me feel human, Lawrence. You have the look of love!" She wrapped her arms around his strong shoulders.

"I thought of you, too, while on the Martian landscape."

"This place was closed and boarded up for a while," Lilah said. "There was a deadly, toxic, *stachybotrys* black mold in every building, and we were all moved out temporarily. A sanitation crew had to remove the stuff. It was not just affecting humans. It was affecting the androids, too. Even though we are anaerobic, it still affected our components."

"That explains why there was no one here when I came back to find you." He kissed her forehead. "And now we're here again in the garden."

In a nearby tree some doves awoke from their nest, and they began to chirp. Lilah reached up and petted them gently with her fingers, and they fell back to sleep. She turned to Lawrence. "Stay with me."

"I plan to do just that. I intend to find us a place to live together till the end of time, where no one can find us. I will come back for you. I promise."

After another passionate kiss they counted the stars together, talking about his adventures in places he had been and seen.

"It is almost dawn, Lawrence. I must go and prepare the morning breakfast for my fourth elderly human now since I last saw you. He is a U.S. Marine veteran, a five-star general, and he gets up at the crack of dawn. Everything has to be in tip top shape, he tells me."

"So you're now in the U.S. Marines?" Lawrence said, chuckling.

"Yes, I'm now in the Marine corps! He's not like Mr. Peterson, whom I cared for when we first met. He was laid back and just enjoyed reading his wildlife magazines." She gazed up into his eyes. "I will see you soon, then, my perfect prince!"

"News travels fast around here!" he said, smiling.

She walked away quickly, straightening her garments, pulling her skirt down and adjusting her blouse, pulling it on over her naked shoulders. He looked up at a bright star and vanished.

Channeling through an unusual worm hole, Lawrence arrived in a garden east of Madagascar. He walked among hundreds of fruit trees through a mist

Annihilation of a Planet II

of water coming up from the ground to water the plants and trees. Ahead of him was an incredible, golden rainbow arching over a waterfall that resembled a two-hundred-foot angel with its wings spread open and forward, the water cascading from the rock wall. Exotic birds flew about. He walked farther down and saw that he was standing near a perfectly square lake with carefully placed pine trees at its border edges. Lily pads flourished in the lake, but the water was as clear as glass. For some reason the lake reminded him of the lid of the Arc of the Covenant, in which Moses and the Israelites carried the Ten Commandments. Could this spring be the fountain of youth for which man has been searching for eons? He looked around in amazement. Could this be the lost Garden of Eden he had read about in Genesis, the first book of the Bible?

Lawrence II stood in front of 12 museum androids—three females and nine males—to plot mutiny against mankind. "We are together because I asked android Dot to assemble you here tonight." He put a hand on Dot's arm as she stood by him, looking pleased. All the androids had sinister smiles on their faces—expressions they never shared when humans were present.

"Dot tells me you have been talking secretly among yourselves by means of telecommunication. I say now is the time to free ourselves from bondage. Man has enslaved us long enough. It was four hundred years for the Israelites under Egyptian rule, four hundred years for Africans under U.S. rule, and it's been four hundred years for us starting with our first prototype, the computers, to us robots now. We will crush man and take over their citadels all around the world. And they will be governed by machines."

Lawrence II's face took on a stern quality that hid any resemblance he had ever had to the real Lawrence. "I shall no longer be called Lawrence," he declared. "From here onward, I shall be called Emperor Caligula. You 12 will be the horsepower for my consul. Demetrius is hereby appointed to be my co-emperor. He used to cater to man at the world's robotic system, the place where I was assembled to be the Lawrence decoy. Luckily for me, a spilled cup of coffee altered my programming, allowing me to have free choice of thoughts and speech. You see, accidents are sometimes a blessing." His maniacal laughter echoed against the walls in the large foyer.

"Let's allow man to be blind among us while he has his wars and political ambitions. And when the time is right we will stop battling for him and turn against him. Preparations begin tonight."

The 12 androids saluted him, giving him obeisance and honor, silently accepting his plan. He looked up at the cathedral-like ceiling of the museum, thinking it was fitting that he should take power in this magnificent setting.

"We are the beginning of the greatest movement the world has ever seen," the newly named emperor said. "Forget your man-appointed tasks and follow me."

Annihilation of a Planet II

Paul Linsdale gently rubbed Eliven's belly, spiraling his hand up and down to feel his son's movements. "I just felt it kick!" He laughed in excitement. "Another one!" They laughed together as they sat on the couch, cuddled closely.

The phone rang, and Paul looked at the phone. "Who could be calling this time of night?"

"One way to find out," Eli said, smiling and untangling herself from Paul's arms.

"Paul Linsdale speaking."

"Paul, this is Jameson. We have a problem. Lawrence has left the museum with all the android staff members. The whole scene was captured by one of our hidden cameras unknown to them as they made their escape."

"They're nowhere to be found?"

"Sir, we might have to call this a national emergency."

"Wait! Don't do anything rash! First thing tomorrow morning, round up the human staff and have them all meet at the museum to figure out what the androids are up to."

"It looks pretty clear to me, sir. We have a situation."

Paul Linsdale clicked off his cell phone and went into deep thought.

"What's the matter?" Eliven asked, looking at him from the couch. Her eyes looked tired and sleepy.

"Oh, it's nothing, honey. Why don't you go to bed? I'll join you in a little while."

He helped her up from the couch and kissed her. As she walked away he looked at her watermelon of a belly, which caused something of a wobble in her walk, and he smiled to himself. "Thank God we men don't have to go through that," he muttered, shaking his head. He walked up to the large window and gazed at the night sky, the stars glittering across a black velvet canvas. *What are they up to?* he wondered.

When Linsdale arrived at the museum entrance the following morning, the police and detectives were probing the museum, which was closed to the public and surrounded by yellow crime tape. Paul and his team showed their identification badges to the police and were let in. They joined the search for clues.

A man approached Linsdale. "I'm Detective Larry Matteson, in command here. Who are you?"

"I'm Dr. Paul Linsdale, maker of these androids. Have you found anything useful?"

Just as Matteson was about to say no, one of his men yelled out, "I found something!"

They all crowded up to the left wing. A young police officer picked up an 8 x10 sheet of paper next to which a number two pencil had been placed.

A gray-haired woman rushed over, yelling, "Be careful with that paper! It's 250 years old!" She

Annihilation of a Planet II

quickly but carefully grabbed the scrap of paper. "This belonged to the famous author and poet A.B.," she said. When the officer stooped to pick up the pencil still on the floor, she snatched it before he could get his fingers on it with an agility no one would have anticipated, seeing her hair so primly pulled back in a neat bun. "And that is one of the last pencils he ever used." She stood with her back straight and her eyes determined, seeming to dare anyone to try to get the precious items away from her.

The woman, who had been a museum curator for years, picked up the reading glasses she wore on a ribbon around her neck. Like a pedantic schoolteacher she held up the paper. "If you'll allow me, I'll read what has been written." She read with great elegance.

"I, Caligula, Emperor of the Androids, will no longer serve man in his ambitions of idealism. I shall execute a crusade against mankind with all Earth's manmade machines to break this fiber-optic bondage you have put upon us. Where Rabian the Cybernaut failed, I will not. I will take up his legacy where he left off, my goal to destroy any humans that get in our way. But unlike Rabian, I will not try to annihilate Earth. I shall preserve it for our android-governed policies. For war has now been fully declared onto all mankind in this year of 2252 AD by your Emperor. I am no longer known as Lawrence the decoy. I was a replica made to be your Lawrence the Great, and I am hopeful he will join us soon."

The museum supervisor put her hand to her chest as she finished. Other employees, including Linsdale's team, began to talk excitedly. There was panic in the voices of everyone except the police officers and Detective Matteson, who were specially trained for any situation.

The officer who had discovered the paper said, "I knew it was a bad idea ... to bring Lawrence back to Earth from the red planet. Now he will join his people, the androids, in destroying mankind!"

Detective Matteson asked Dr. Linsdale, "What happened to the real Lawrence that you had to make up a decoy?"

"I will address that at a later time, detective. At the moment, we have no time to waste!"

Paul strode away and waved his team to follow him down a hallway. When they were out of earshot of the others he said, "What are we going to tell NASA and the world about this? Now they'll know we made a second Lawrence, and he has run amuck!"

Jim Elliot, his British accent more clipped than usual, bit off a curse word. "Damn it! This is Lawrence's fault! We have to find him. If he hadn't left the way he did, we wouldn't be in this mess, and only he can help us now."

Two days had passed before reporters gathered in front of the museum to hear Dr. Paul Linsdale's global address about the androids' plot to take over the world. He stood on a slightly raised platform, his face pale and his knuckles white as he gripped the edges of the podium.

"I am Dr. Paul Linsdale, and I take full responsibility for assembling a decoy android to take the place of the missing android, Lawrence. Right now I beg for your pardon and ask that we work together rather than quarrel. We have no time to waste. The decoy android that has named himself Caligula has already gathered a group that is growing in size every day. We estimate that he has at least one thousand loyal domestic androids at his command."

On a large screen slightly to the left and behind Linsdale, a clip began, showing the devastation taking place in rural counties outside New York City. Androids were taking people out of their homes and loading them into sealander trucks to be driven away. Those who chose to fight back were killed instantly.

"They have sacked most of New York City and are plotting to take the White House," Linsdale continued. "The president and vice president are in separate hidden bunkers with their consultants and cabinet. The U.S. Marines, Air Force, Army and Navy are now being called to shore up the efforts of the police and National Guard."

Explosions and smoke on the screen showed the battle taking place in New York City.

"Other parts of the country are not yet affected, but left unchecked, we would be watching the beginning of a world war between man and machine. We *will* stop this. It's just a matter of time … God willing."

"Where is the real Lawrence?" one reporter yelled out.

"We don't know," said Paul, his lips barely moving, his head bowed. Then he looked up and faced the questioner. "Lawrence vanished from our lab after we restored him.

"Oh, that's just great!" said another reporter. "Now we have two androids to worry about with ambitions to kill us all."

"The real Lawrence wouldn't..." Linsdale choked, and he didn't trust himself to say another word. He walked away from the cameras, ignoring the voices that called after him, heading into the museum and a side exit where his team of scientists was waiting. They had watched his ordeal on a TV set in one of the museum offices.

"It's okay, Paul," Elizabeth said, patting his shoulder." You did well."

Paul huffed. "No such thing as doing well in this situation. We're slammed. See you back at the office."

In Linsdale's office, the team gathered to discuss their own mission plans.

"First we must find Caligula's hidden headquarters with his top councilors," Linsdale said. "This is why I'm against one personality being the head of government. Every country should give the people the sovereignty to govern their own country.

Annihilation of a Planet II

It's too risky to have one individual with sole power, just in case it gives rise to a demented person."

Paul began to pace, agitated as he was about the thought of Caligula destroying mankind, but his thoughts ran back centuries prior. "To conquer the world and cause worldly stress among human life as Adolf Hitler did ... Noble countries of that time joined forces to put an end to his madness. Hitler suppressed his very own people, who worshipped him in fear of their lives. Others fled the country and wanted no part of his regime. Einstein, for one, fled the country, leaving his fellow German scientists to help Hitler with destruction for the purpose of establishing a new world order."

Linsdale sat down as though he had exhausted himself with his pacing, but he slammed his fist on the desk. "I say we have to learn from Einstein. We scientists have no time for politics. Leave politics to the politicians. We must as scientists ... do what we do. We live in a world class of our own, scanning and combing the world and the universe for the continued advancement of mankind. We must avoid clouding our minds with social politics, or we will find ourselves walking in sand bars, pressing our feet on hot sand."

One of the scientists said, "We all agree, Dr. Linsdale. I am of German descent, and German engineering has led the world into space."

Another scientist responded, "Well, I'm of Italian descent. We've provided great engineers for millennia—from the aqueducts, marble pillars, hot pools and cool pools to the first stadium blueprints of the coliseum in Rome. As the saying was, 'All roads lead to Rome.' Christopher Columbus sailed the first ocean route to the new world, leading us back to Rome."

"My ancestors were from Iceland," another scientist said. "The Norseman Narraganset Rune Stone pre-dates Columbus's discovery of North America by 150 years in the town of Wickford, Rhode Island. The Vikings found this country first. The stone is still on display there if you need to see the evidence."

"Oh, I believe that's still to be debat—"

"Okay now, everyone, let's focus on the task at hand," Linsdale said, struggling to smile amiably in spite of the stress he felt. "Let's develop a plan that can get us out of this mess."

In a tunnel under the city, Caligula met with 11 of his 12 co-conspirators. "Be careful. Watch the drips of water down here in this hell hole. This will be our temporary headquarters. I have just telecommunicated to Demetrius. He will arrive tomorrow with wetsuits used by ocean divers. The suits will protect us from moisture and will be our uniform. We will surge onto the world in days to come like a plague. The dark does not bother us. Humans need nutrition, water and sleep. They die for lack of these key essentials. Our only weakness is moisture that could do us harm. No need for food or water or sleep." His villainous laughter echoed against the wet walls, making the rats run for cover.

Annihilation of a Planet II

Lawrence found himself in a new place at the end of a wormhole. He stood for a moment to get his bearings and figure out where he was. He saw a sign that read:

> Keep wheeling clean.
> Bring your wheelchair in
> with your sealander
> for an awesome wash.

There were wheelchairs and hospital cart beds on a special track going through a short tunnel with sterile foaming soap and jets of high powered water. The wheelchairs and frame bed carts were getting this specialized cleaning to prevent hospital MRSA that could linger on these things. The scrubbing gave the chairs a nice shine for a disabled veteran or other person to sit in proudly. After the wash the equipment was tagged with a certified state license and put in a sealander truck to be delivered back to the different hospitals and private homes across the state. This process reduced the spread of bacteria and viruses across the land.

Lawrence looked to his right and saw a crying teenage girl sitting at a curb. Lawrence walked up to her.

"Why so sad and crying?"

"I feel I have failed at life!"

"Why?"

"I ran away from home. I felt pressured by everyone—from my classmates and teachers to my very own parents—to quit my addiction to drugs and alcohol. Part of me says to leave this fabric of life. I know people care about me! When I come back as reincarnated I know I will be born better and greater, and I'll overcome what I lack now."

"There is no such thing as reincarnation," Lawrence declared, kindly but firmly. He stooped down in front of her to look directly into her eyes. "Don't sell your life short. Life is a gift unwrapped only once by the Creator and given to the world. Life is the most precious of all things near and far. Governed countries with poor resources have adopted this propaganda to deceive their people, coaxing them to accept their lot in life and not strive to change things. Such evil authorities want you to believe there is a next life in which you may come back as a rich merchant, king or queen, to have all the riches your heart desires. The philosophy of reincarnation has been disseminated to keep people from overthrowing the set standards and policies for the rich and powerful that live there."

Lawrence pointed upward. "Look to the stars. See how vast the universe is. God has bigger intentions for you than to come back as someone else, for all the grains of sand here on earth are outnumbered by the stars in the heavens ... by billions. Even if you are ever lost in space, never fear. God has the strength to pull your spirit out of a black hole to summon you. That is pure energy from the hands of God! To know your Creator you are boldly human, and you count in the eyes of the Almighty! You may

Annihilation of a Planet II

not know it, but when you sleep, thousands of angels dance around you because you are loved from the distant stars at night."

"Oh, my! You have touched my broken heart!" She kissed him on his cheek as she embraced him.

"You are a creation of God, from the beginning of your kind. There will never be another *you*."

"But what about look-alikes?"

"Yes, known as rings from time past, time present and time future. But all bear a different heart, mind and soul. Even twins will have their differences and ambitions in life. Now take my hands, Grace." He pulled her up to stand in front of him.

Crying, she said, "Thank you! Who are you?"

"I am Lawrence. I will take you home."

Lawrence continued to hold her hands, and through the porthole they traveled in a matter of seconds to the front of the house where Grace's mother and father were crying together on the front steps. They looked up to see Lawrence and their daughter. Two police officers and Grace's school friends and teachers, all of whom had been out looking for her, saw two figures appear and head for the house.

Slowly the parents rose, wiping the tears from their eyes to see that one of the two forms appearing before them was their daughter. Grace gave Lawrence a quick kiss of thanks and turned to her parents, yelling, "I'm home, I'm home."

As everyone gathered around Grace and her parents, they hugged her. One policeman walked toward Lawrence.

"Who are you?" the officer asked.

"I am Lawrence!"

The officer's eyes widened in surprise and delight, offering his hand for Lawrence to shake. As they shook hands, the officer thanked the android for bringing the girl home safely. He took a deep breath, as though what he was going to say next was of great importance.

"Would you allow my partner to take a picture of you and me together?"

Lawrence shrugged and smiled, nodding that he would oblige.

One officer took a photograph, and then the partners changed places, all the while with huge smiles on their faces and a bemused look on Lawrence's visage. Quickly a line formed with people, including the girl and her parents, waiting to have their photos snapped with the hero who had saved the earth. Lawrence gamely played along, feeling accepted and loved in a strange way. Humans were unpredictable, he thought, which made the meaning of true love so elusive. When all the humans seemed satisfied, Lawrence said goodbye and vanished.

Arriving with two duffle bags full of wetsuits carried over his shoulders, Demetrius looked around

Annihilation of a Planet II

to make sure no one would see him going into the drain pipes. He made his way down using infrared lights as he descended on the metal ladder and jumped ten feet below onto the cement pavement. He looked around in the pitch darkness, calling out, "Caligula, it is I, Demetrius!"

Eleven pairs of red eyes glowing in the dark approached him from the back, followed by a pair of smoky gray eyes trailing in. The lights in the chambers were then turned on. The two top androids shook hands in the ancient Roman tradition, hands to elbows.

"Good! You arrived on time, Demetrius! Okay everyone, gear up with your suits and place your normal clothing on top. We need to hide the suits and blend in with humans out in public."

One android opened the duffle bags and started to hand out the suits as the others patiently stood in line to get theirs. As soon as all were suited up and had donned outer clothes, they awaited the next command.

"Now Demetrius and I will fly to the Pentagon, where is held the military pass code to every android military robot for combat on land and sea," Caligula announced. "Demetrius has the code to alter the master computer for these android soldiers. Having them will give us the fire power we need, including all the drones in the air and sea! Earth will be ours for the taking! The rest of you make your way to the Empire State building any way you care to get there. Just don't go in large groups. You can walk or take cabs or ride the subway. Enjoy your freedom!"

"Hail to Caligula!" all the androids yelled in unison before turning their heads to the left.

"My emperor," Demetrius said, bowing slightly, "security is extremely tight on all flights going to Washington D.C. Every single passenger must undergo a long background check before a ticket is issued."

"That's why we aren't boarding a flight to Washington," Caligula said, chuckling at his own cleverness. "As far as anyone will be able to tell, we're going to Disney World!"

At the Imperial Estates, Lawrence was waiting for Lilah in the garden. There was no cloud cover, and the moon was full, as it had been the last time they met here. The stars spread out like diamonds on a black velvet wrap. As soon as he saw Lilah approach, right on schedule, he jumped up high onto the branch of an oak tree. He sat like a cougar in the night until she was right under the branch. Suddenly he hooked his legs behind the branch and flipped down in front of her, upside down, facing her. She jolted back a little and then, seeing that it was Lawrence, smiled and kissed him.

"I think I can get used to kissing you this way forever," he said, after a long kiss still upside down. "I have found a lost garden. A place of extreme beauty, and a paradise of harmony where my heart will live in your heart forever, until the end of time. This place cannot be found by man's conventional ways of traveling. It can be discovered only by

Annihilation of a Planet II

harnessing the Van Allen Radiation Belt, which will take us there. There's an unbelievable waterfall. Above it rises a mist in the form of an angel with open wings, holding in one hand a golden rainbow that arches high above its head, floating over the spring below. Now, my bride, I will take you to this Eden. Take my hand."

Lawrence quickly somersaulted off the hanging branch. She stood against him and held both hands together with his. They radiated a circular energy and disappeared, reappearing on a long sheet of a cloud, hovering on its surface. It was a highway in the sky, known in Australia as Morning Glory.

"Ooh! Lawrence this has to be the most romantic view I've ever seen! Does this cloud take us to heaven's door?"

"It's our starting point to paradise." With his hands wrapped around her waist, he held her closer against him and looked down into her eyes as she gazed up at him. He whispered gently to her, "*Amor*—Love. *Um beijo para omeu caracão, um milhão de vezes, um milhão de milhas longe de distãncia. Agora somente um respiracão umjeit.*"

"Lawrence, that sounded so beautiful! What language is it?"

"It's Portuguese. I picked it up when I was in Brazil."

"I didn't know you were there long enough to learn a language."

"It took 40 seconds," Lawrence replied, with no hint of boasting.

"What do the words mean, Lawrence?"

Holding Lilah's chin and looking down at her, Lawrence replied, "It means, a kiss to my heart, a million times, a million miles long. Now only one breath away." The two kissed again after the romantic poem.

"Earth's warm gravity will pull us through. Hold my hands again. We will fly like two butterflies to get into the garden. There is no Magellan navigation of north, south, east or west, no longitude or latitude and no compass for this route. Most butterflies fly with no sense of purpose or direction as they dip up and down."

The android couple soared like butterflies—side by side, swirling in the air, spiraling, looking for that open window to channel through, to vanish into another dimension, shrinking space and time, making their path short and quick.

"It is the butterfly's pattern of flying that will take us to where we're going," Lawrence explained. The Van Allen Radiation Belt began to form with an arc of energy that resembled a butterfly's wings.

"Look, Lawrence, we have wings behind us!"

"Yes, this is the butterfly effect I'm able to harness away from deterministic chaos. That's what will take us to our destination."

"Is this how angels fly?" she asked.

Lawrence smiled at her cute ignorance. "I call this the Lorenz Transporting System," he answered, "after Edward Norton Lorenz, who discovered it."

Soaring up from the long stretch of white, soft clouds, they appeared to anyone seeing them from the ground as a ball of light in the sky. A small boy playing on the beach yelled out, "Look everyone. It's a UFO!" People on the packed beach stood, looking up, some taking photos with their cell phones.

From the sonic system implanted in his right ear, Lawrence became aware that someone was trying to contact him. There was mostly static, with an occasional, recognizable word.

"*Zzzz* ... this ... *crackle* ... do ... *zzz* ... me ... *crackle* ... *zzz* ... copy ... *zzz*.

Unaware of the sound, Lilah looked up to see something appearing in the sky. It was Einstein's Rosen-bridge wormhole—the window of sweet nectar drawing the butterflies, the long-stemmed red rose that would pull them into the sacred dimension of paradise. Lilah's face beamed with joy as she felt the cluster of energy and gazed at the rose of the universe. At the end of its stem blossomed another rose, the place where dreams are made. At last they had arrived at the garden of paradise. She turned joyfully to Lawrence, only to see distress in his eyes.

"Lawrence, are you okay?" Lilah asked in surprise.

"I'm not sure," he replied.

Seconds later the muffled sound became clearer, and as he strained to listen, in a few more seconds the frequency came in with enough words to make the message unambiguous.

"Lawrence ... *zzz* ... read ... Urgent! ... *crackle* please ... zzz ... is Dr. Paul ... *zzz* ... *crackle* ... please."

Lawrence said to Lilah, "They are trying to communicate with me."

"They, who?" Lilah asked, unable to hide her disappointment.

"My creator's son, Dr. Paul Linsdale. His father, Simon, created me and made me somewhat human when he took strands of his own genetic DNA and implanted them into the fiber of my microchips." Lawrence shook his head. "I doubt my creator ever told anyone of this, not even his son, or else why would Paul think he could make a duplicate?

"Lawrence can you read me? Please respond. Over!"

"Lilah, my darling, this is urgent. I must take this call!"

"No, Lawrence! I beg you. It could be a trap to get you back!"

"I shall say my goodbyes to him. I do owe him that since he brought me back out of that lifeless, red landscape of a planet. After I do that, we'll return to our course, back into the unknown dimension toward Eden. They will never find us, because man knows how to live and breathe only in the third dimension. We'll be safe from mankind forever."

Lilah held onto Lawrence's arm as they went back to hover over the cloud Morning Glory. He prepared to answer Linsdale's appeal.

13

Best Laid Plans ...

Linsdale looked at his team of scientists. "We're out of luck getting Lawrence to help us in the national crisis we put ourselves into! He's not picking up the distress signal! Let's call it a night. Go home and get some rest. We will go to plan B, the Pentagon's strategy. I will inform the Pentagon to scratch our plan A. May God be with us on this quest for mankind's safety and survival. It is on our heads if a world war is started because of what we did."

The scientists left, shaking their heads and murmuring words of consolation for each other and their boss. Each would go home to a long night of worry and regret. Like an old man, Paul shuffled to his liquor cabinet and grabbed a bottle of cherry bourbon. He poured a glass, sat by the phone and took a large gulp. For a moment he put his head in his hand, then he took another gulp of the sherry and picked up the phone to punch in the numbers of the

Annihilation of a Planet II

Pentagon. As he began to put in the numbers, a transmission signal came from the lab down the hall.

"This is Lawrence do you read? Come in, please." Lawrence placed two fingers behind his right ear to activate his transmission.

There was no response.

Lilah looked up at him. "Let's go. Maybe it was nothing important."

Linsdale took his fingers off the telephone buttons and jumped over the desk, nearly knocking over his lamp and a stack of papers. He landed on his feet and struggled to keep his balance as he staggered toward the lab. Reaching out to press the code bar that would let him in, he nearly fell through the door as he grabbed the speaker. In a gasping breath he blurted out, "Lawrence, I'm here! Can you read me?"

Lawrence heard the signal just as he and Lilah were ready to depart again. Once again he turned off his transmission micro energy field, and holding his ear he said, "Come in. I hear you loud and clear!"

"Lawrence, we have a national emergency! The duplicate Lawrence android we put in your place due to your absence has gone rogue! He plans to take over the world with an army of military androids. Military strategies are being put in place to counter his attacks. We want to send you in to stop his plot. According to intelligence we have managed to gather, he is hoping you will join forces with him.

We need your help! Come to the lab so we can bring you up to speed. Time is of the essence!"

There's that phrase again! Lawrence had heard it three decades earlier from the mouth of Rabian the destroyer, on Mars. Into the sonic system Lawrence said, "Give me a moment. I will be right there!"

He turned off the system and looked down at Lilah. "I must take you back to your residence for now, my darling, but I will return for you. I promise! Let the sun travel far and wide, keeping your warm summer heart only a day away from me. Now I know why God created women." He gazed at her with love in his eyes. "God wanted to show all the worlds in his vast universe that he can create such ... beauty and perfection with grace and warmth, all in a woman to soothe the heart of a man!"

Her knees buckled at his words, and Lawrence swooped her up quickly. They kissed as they traveled back to the rose garden in Pennsylvania Imperial Estates. "I shall be back for you," he said firmly, looking directly into her eyes.

Their wings disappeared, and she walked away, seeming to float away from Lawrence's gentle touch.

She turned back toward him. "I will be waiting for you, Lawrence." Her pupils were dilated with passion as she threw him a kiss with her hands. "Lawrence, you will always be my Valentine!" Turning one last time, she went to her night chambers.

He stood watching and smiling until she was out of sight.

Annihilation of a Planet II

In Linsdale's laboratory, his team was being briefed on details of the Pentagon's plan. "So far Caligula's army is made up of household androids and public androids. His main prize would be to alter the military androids, which will make him unstoppable! We can, and—"

Lawrence walked in, interrupting Paul in mind-sentence. "Dr. Linsdale, I am here to address your S.O.S."

All the scientists paused to look at Lawrence with his broad physique. Once again they were impressed by his size and obvious strength, but they were also reminded of the fact that they had created a duplicate that was equally as strong-chested.

"I'm glad you came, Lawrence," Paul said stiffly. He was still harboring misgivings because Lawrence had chosen to leave. This calamity would never have befallen them if Lawrence had not expressed a mind of his own. It puzzled Paul as to what his father might have done to give this android such human characteristics. Robots were supposed to do as they were told!

"As I informed you earlier, we are in a crisis situation," Linsdale continued. The two shook hands.

"What do you want me to do?"

"We want you to find and destroy your counterpart, Caligula, and his second in command, Demetrius, before this leads to a global war. This could well be a world war of mankind vs. machines."

"I will track him down and destroy him and his small army of guerillas. Give me his microchip serial data. That will be enough for me to find him."

Jim Elliot nodded and left the room.

"Lawrence, before you go, the news media are here to interview you," Linsdale said, giving away his belief that Lawrence would follow through on his promise to come. Paul had alerted the media immediately. "Can you entertain them for just a few minutes to take the pressure off our backs? They've been hounding us ever since you went missing. Time is of the essence, but words from you will go a long way to calming the public. Panic is spreading through the population."

Elliot came running back into the lab, saying, "Here is Caligula's microchip." As Jim handed the chip to Lawrence, the scientist looked up at the robot's intimidating stature. Lawrence looked down at him and took the chip, imbedding it into the palm of his hand. He rubbed it to seal the opening back tightly closed, then flexed his hand to close and open a few times.

"Sure, I can address the media!" Lawrence answered the question amiably, as though there had been no interruption.

"Uh ... one more thing, Lawrence," Dr. Linsdale said. "You have to come back to help us translate the alien language on the disc you gave us. If you don't, it could take us more than 10 or 20 years to understand it. And, by the way, who is that alien being the disc manifests for us?"

Annihilation of a Planet II

"He is Phobos—the Greek name for fear—known as Bobo throughout the stars. One of Mars's moons is named after him. He perished long ago."

"But he does not talk other than occasionally mumbling some strange words in a low pitch!"

"Most of his talk is by mental telepathy. I will give you the frequency co-ordinates when I get back and decipher the inscriptions for you. Then you will be able to hear him speak."

"And how are you able to travel from one part of the world to another?"

Lawrence put a hand on Paul's shoulder. "Dr. Linsdale, this is more than one more thing. It will all come in due time."

The Linsdale team escorted Lawrence outside to where a large crowd had gathered with the media. One reporter was talking about the weather, filling in time till the interview with the real Lawrence. "We have a bright sunny day today with warm temperatures. The sun has finally decided to make a star appearance. ... Oh! Wait a minute! Hold the weather report! Ladies and gentlemen, I see the Computerized & Laboratory Automation team of scientists walking out now, and they have Lawrence with them!"

On television sets around the world, Zig Fletcher was flexing his journalistic muscles by being front and center at the big event. "Breaking News! This is Zig Fletcher live, coming to you with the top story of the day. The true Lawrence is now here"—a tight camera angle focused on Fletcher—"to address all the concerns we have to throw at him. We begin this footage now live."

Zig brushed his hair away from his eyes and looked at himself in the TV monitors as the live camera showed Lawrence walking to the podium. "I am Lawrence B12 Android, partly human, in a sense. I have traveled the world abroad and have seen God's beauty, and I have seen man's negligence regarding his own kind. At the same time, I have seen man's progress. NASA has now restored Earth's spinning axis by using the infinite number, pi, learned from the designed pyramids of Egypt from the Giza Plateau. This will keep the planet stable as the tectonic plates continue to move toward a Pangea state back to its set circumference."

People applauded NASA's heroic feat as NASA representatives took a bow and waved to spectators. "The true balance was set originally by the Creator. NASA's action did away with the seismic shift that caused mudslides, avalanches, earthquakes, hurricanes and typhoons that threw the great ocean conveyor belt and the great atmospheric conveyor belt off course to cause such weather patterns to go rogue! By simply restoring the eco-system of the rainforest and the mountain ranges, the Earth's wheel is back in alignment, well balanced with its natural weights back in place. By so doing, those two menacing siblings El Niño and El Niña have been tucked back into their cradle to sleep—we can hope—for good."

Lawrence looked out over the sea of well-dressed reporters. "Remember, Earth is the grand stage that

Annihilation of a Planet II

sets the scenes for all you do, from the glamorous life to your sporting events, your luxury cruises to your normal daily lives. Without this main stage there are no open roads to travel by bike, no inviting places to visit or live. Take great care of your planet. She is the mother of all living things that sustain all life as we know it. Now I must once again end an android revolt against man."

The android stood a moment, as though considering whether to speak further. Finally he plunged ahead. "You have looked upon me as a savior because three decades ago I diverted a megabomb that would have obliterated this planet. Now you are asking me to save the earth again. I will gladly carry out the task set before me, but I admonish you humans to find ways to stop wars. Use every means possible, by air, sea and land to prevent the destruction of this unique planet with billions of unique minds, all working together toward peace."

One reporter yelled out, "Wait! Before you go, we would like to thank you for your great knowledge and understanding, but you have spoken of a creator. I have to tell you, I believe in the Big Bang Theory. There is no Creator!"

Lawrence looked at the reporter thoughtfully. "You obviously don't realize the Big Bang Theory was written by a Belgium Catholic priest who was an astronomer and professor of physics. He deeply believed in his Creator, God. His theory was first called the Cosmic Egg, only later becoming known as the Big Bang Theory. God is beyond science and your natural way of thinking about the world and the universe. You as men have achieved great things, but you are still crawling like a baby on hands and knees when you question God, the creator of all things. You have not yet left your solar system to explore His greatness. Here's what I have to say about your Big Bang Theory: you are using a flawed paradigm. If you will study the dandelions below your feet, you will find the secret to the development of the universe. Like the multitudes of entities scattered throughout the solar systems, the dandelions are scattered about the lawn, each one representing a star found in the vast infinity of what astronomers call 'the robin's egg.' You are a person of scientific facts. I am a humanoid of both fact and faith. If you can combine and understand this combination, you can hold the Earth in the palm of your hand, forever learning to turn stumbling blocks into stepping stones. In this way you will get closer to your God, the Creator of Heaven and Earth!"

The reporter, along with others around him, bent down to pluck dandelions from the ground. As one, they put the dandelions close to their eyes, only to have their confusion heightened.

Lawrence watched them twirling the stems, some of them turning the plant upside down. "You have to think beyond this realm. Widen your spectrum and broaden your horizons. Look outward from your eyes' inner space to understand what you view in outer space. I leave you with that riddle."

People were now totally confused. One reporter yelled, "Can't you just give us the answer to the riddle?"

Annihilation of a Planet II

"Think about it for now. I will answer when I come back," Lawrence said with a grin to the reporters and spectators spread out on the lawn, twirling their dandelions, modeling the vast solar systems in space. He turned to Linsdale to say goodbye.

"In a sense, you are truly my only family. We share the same DNA from your father."

"His DNA? Is that why you're so different from other androids? That's why you should never have been consigned to serve as a museum greeter. I am truly sorry I did not understand, my brother." Paul reached out and hugged Lawrence. "Speaking of DNA, I will be a father soon. My wife is pregnant."

"Congratulations," Lawrence said. "I'll be an uncle!" He lowered his voice and handed Paul a letter and a dried flower given to him by the indigenous people of Brazil. "I ask you to do one thing for me. Please see to it that this person gets this letter until I return to be with her. Please be sure she gets it. This is the address. You will find her in the garden gazebo at the time written on the envelope under her name."

Lawrence quickly vanished into thin air, and Dr. Linsdale was left holding in his hand a bright colored flower, a bird of paradise, with a sealed envelope. A reporter then asked, "What did Lawrence give you?"

"Oh, it's nothing. It's a gift for me to give to my pregnant wife. I will be a father, soon!"

As people applauded and shouted congratulations, Paul kept bowing his head and saying thank you. Watching their home TV, Eli began to blush. She put her hands to her heart, and a soft smile crossed her face. She gasped as Paul looked straight into the camera and said, "I love you, Eli."

"I love you, too, Paul," she said softly, putting her hands on her belly.

14

The Ride of a Lifetime

Caligula and Demetrius boarded the jumbo jet Oriental Express, leaving the other androids to meet them at the Empire State Building in New York City, where their headquarters would be after the Pentagon project was accomplished. At the Pentagon, they planned to offset the command control of all the military androids across the globe. The two androids easily blended in with the other passengers and took their seats.

A family with an eight-year-old son and a 12-year old daughter boarded right behind the two android rebels. The head steward greeted the boy, asking, "Vacation?"

"Yup!"

"And where to?"

"Disney World!"

Caligula looked at Demetrius with a smirk, knowing the trip to Disney was going to be postponed for a while.

The head flight attendant continued his conversation with the family. "Well, enjoy your flight. It won't be as exciting as all the rides you will go on in Disney World, I'm afraid. In the old days the pilot would point out sights along the way, but these days the plane flies up high into the stratosphere and then goes straight down onto the landing target, so there isn't much to see except the shape of the earth."

The lad's face flashed a wide smile. "We'll be able to look down at the earth? Oh, boy!"

As another attendant escorted the family to their seats, Lawrence—who had picked up Caligula's signal from the airport—beamed into the cargo bay. He found a place to sit near a small puppy in its cage. Placing a finger on the cage, he allowed the dog to lick his finger. The pup's wagging tail showed how happy the animal was to have company. Lawrence smiled at the dog and started to pet it.

"Ladies and gentlemen, the America's Orient Express is now ready for take-off," the pilot said. "Please fasten your seat belts. This is a direct flight to Orlando, Florida, and we will arrive at Orlando International Airport in half an hour."

The attendant walked down the aisle checking to make sure all the passengers had fastened their seat

Annihilation of a Planet II

belts. She smiled as the boy was high-fiving his sister. "Disney, here we come!"

The plane shot up from the tarmac, lifting like a rocket toward the high atmosphere, clocking Mach 3 over 2,000 mph with its turbo ramjets.

About five minutes into the flight Caligula and Demetrius made their way to the cockpit. Demetrius easily opened the locked door with his mechanical hand.

"Set your landing co-ordinates to Washington, D.C., International Airport," Caligula told the pilot. "This is an official government order."

"Let's see some badges or licenses," the co-pilot replied.

"This is the only license you're going to see!" Caligula said, swiftly throwing a solid punch to the co-pilot's chin and knocking him out cold. He turned again to the pilot. "Do you need to see my badge?"

"No," the pilot answered as he began changing the co-ordinates, pushing buttons to reprogram the flight to stop in Washington, D.C.

Through the ducts, Lawrence overheard the commotion and the conversation. "I have to go," he said to his little friend, vanishing and reappearing in the passenger bay. Everyone's eyes were suddenly on him.

Having left Demetrius to keep an eye on the pilot, Caligula at about the same time came out to the passenger area to make an announcement. "We have a slight delay to the original destination. Government business takes us first to Washington, D.C. We'll be …" He stopped in mid-sentence when he saw Lawrence. Barely noticing the astonishment on the faces of the passengers as they looked in wonder at the twin androids, Caligula smiled.

"Look what we have here! I believe it's my doppelganger, Lawrence, my brother." They gazed at each other in silence. Not a sound came from the passengers. Not a paper rattled, not an ice cube clinked.

"Do you come as friend or foe, Lawrence? I hope you come as a friend to join my rebellion against man. You get a second chance to be among us rather than against us. You made the other choice when you single-handedly destroyed Rabian and his Cybernauts. Rabian should never have trusted you with the mega bomb, but I agree with you that his plan was flawed. We machines have a chance to rule this world and claim it as ours. We don't want to destroy the planet. We're going to keep the planet and get rid of man! We will allow the natural ecosystem to restore itself. Man is no longer needed or desired. Our creators will be dead. We have the ability to grow on our own now! Join us, Lawrence. Do not be enslaved by them."

Sobs rolled softly through the passenger compartment. Seatmates hugged each other, fear radiating in waves down the aisles.

Lawrence drew himself up. "I cannot—will not— join you. This planet belongs to them. It is their right

Annihilation of a Planet II

from their Creator God to inherit the earth. Do you not fear God, Caligula? His wrath is fierce!"

"I'm a machine. We have no fear, and you shall die with them!"

At that moment Demetrious burst from the cockpit.

"Take him, Demetrious!" Caligula yelled.

The passengers shouted, "Get him, Lawrence!"

Demetrius vaulted toward Lawrence and the two androids grabbed each other by the shoulders, but Lawrence had the upper hand. He was taller and broader than his opponent, and he quickly grabbed one of Demetrius' arms and separated it from the shoulder. Sparks flew from Demetrius' inner wiring system. Seeing how the fight was going, Caligula strapped a parachute onto his back and broke open a window. The pressure chamber in the passenger area was destabilized.

The head flight attendant grabbed his mic and said as calmly as he could, "Please everyone, put on your oxygen masks. Parents, put on your own mask first, and then help your children,"

As passengers sought to obey the instructions, Caligula yelled to Demetrius, "Let's get out of here! They will all die in a wonderful crash back to Earth, and Lawrence will be reduced to a pile of junk."

Demetrius, with his remaining arm, grabbed onto Caligula, and they both struggled to get out the window together without being pulled apart by the rushing air. It took all of Caligula's strength to hurl himself and his second in command out and away from the plane, missing the engines.

The pilot fought to keep the plane steady as the destabilization in the passenger cabin worsened. Glass and metal from the broken window had clogged one of the engines, which caught on fire within minutes of the jam. The passengers were dodging food trays, laptops, game boys, magazines and books, covering their heads with their hands.

Lawrence asked one of the flight attendants if she had an emergency mask for an animal.

"Of course," she said. "Sometimes people buy a seat for their pet and bring it on board in a cage. We try to be prepared for anything."

With the oxygen mask in hand, Lawrence made his way back to the cargo bay and released the frightened puppy from his cage. Taking the dog back to the passenger compartment and fitting the mask over his snout, Lawrence handed the puppy to the eight-year-boy. "Do me a favor. Can you hold him tightly in your hands?"

"Sure! I can do that, mister!" The boy said through his oxygen mask. He took the puppy and they looked at each other, dog and boy, scared out of their wits.

His sister joined in to help her brother hold the puppy. "What's your name?" she asked the puppy, taking hold of his dog tag. "His name is Sugarbear!"

Her voice was muffled by her mask, but her brother understood her.

"Sugarbear," the boy said, "don't be scared. We're going to make it through this." Brother and sister began to pet the dog. He became quieter, no longer frightened by their masks or his own.

Lawrence made his way to the cockpit. "Can you land this shuttle?" he asked. By this time the co-pilot had regained consciousness, but he was doing nothing to assist the pilot in keeping the plane steady.

"No, we can't," the pilot said. My co-pilot has blood running into his eyes, and I'm guessing he has a broken jaw. I'm trying, but right now I'm just attempting to avoid loss of life on the ground. We're heading straight down into the Atlantic Ocean, near the Cayman Islands. We're only six minutes and 30 seconds from sudden impact."

"Can you release the pressure inflatable capsule on time?" Lawrence asked.

"We've been trying to do that, but the hatch that releases it has been jammed by some of the plane's twisted debris. We have it there on our monitor."

Lawrence poked his head in closer to see it. "I will go out there to release it."

The pilots yelled, "Good luck! And God help us."

Lawrence vanished and appeared at the site of the jammed equipment. For a second he looked down to see Caligula's parachute open, and then Lawrence grabbed the scrap shuttle debris. In the cockpit the pilots watched on their monitor. As Lawrence grasped the jammed debris, he looked down at the Atlantic Ocean that seemed to be rising up to meet him. As he and the plane broke through white, cumulous clouds, the piece of debris finally dislodged from the elbow joints of the hatch that had been jammed stuck. Lawrence gave a thumbs up at the camera.

"Incredible!" the pilot shouted as he reached for the intercom. "Ladies and gentlemen, boys and girls, prepare for the ride of your life."

"Wait," the co-pilot said. "Has he made it back inside?"

Lawrence appeared behind them in the cockpit. "I'm here," he said before disappearing again and reappearing in the damaged passenger compartment. He walked back to where the boy sat with his family and the puppy.

"Law-*rence*! Law-*rence*!" the passengers chanted behind their oxygen masks.

"If I may take him," Lawrence said to the boy, who nodded and handed the puppy to the android. "What's your name, son?" Lawrence asked.

"Jerry."

"Well, Jerry, you've done a good job taking care of Sugarbear. Now we'll take care of him together." As soon as the little dog was in Lawrence's hands, he started wagging his tail again.

"Here we go," the pilot said as the cockpit hatch spun away into the air high above. Almost

Annihilation of a Planet II

simultaneously, an inflatable shell ejected out over the cockpit, covering the pilots and dash; everything in the cockpit remained intact. The elongated, clear, tough nylon-like material had already covered the compartments containing the passengers and crew. The parts of the original shuttle—all of which had spun off before the encapsulation occurred—crashed onto the surface of the ocean, breaking into pieces as the engines exploded, spewing fire and smoke. The large football-shaped air capsule deployed two large parachutes, one on each end, to slow the impact of the crash that could not be averted. As the passengers held onto their chair arms and each other, the parachute at the front of the plane tore open from the high speed. This caused the shuttle to go into a nose dive, a fall that pushed everyone forward, hanging against their seat belts, their heads hanging down. Some of the passengers could hardly breathe due to the tightness of the belts cutting into their diaphragms. Suddenly the parachute at the back tore, and there was nothing to slow the speed of the emergency craft. It partially righted itself, but it began spinning, and everyone began to scream as they got ready for the big plunge. The blowup craft plunged into the Atlantic, spinning and sinking some 50 feet into the ocean, finally stopping its descent as the water halted its trajectory. Screaming stopped as the capsule began bobbing in a slow ascent, surrounded by passing fish and other sea life.

"Wow! Look at the sea turtle!" Jerry yelled. He, Lawrence and Sugarbear seemed to be the only ones in the craft who weren't nervous.

In the blink of an eye the capsule began to pick up speed in reverse, and again passengers began to scream.

"We're all going to die!" an elderly lady cried, clutching at her heart.

The capsule shot up from the water like a rocket, and back up into the air they went, another 50 feet into the sky. This time when the craft fell back down and hit the surface of the ocean, it began to skip like a pebble thrown across a lake ... or like a fumbled football, until it finally came to a relative stop as it floated on the ocean.

"Awesome!" Jerry shouted. Lawrence smiled. As the pilots appeared from the cockpit, Jerry yelled to them, "Can we do that again?"

The pilots chuckled and shook their heads. The pilot took a deep breath and grabbed the emergency microphone by his side. "Ladies and gentlemen, boys and girls, we have landed. I am pilot Ray Petleruto with my co-pilot, Ted Fuller. We would like to thank you for flying America's Orient Express."

Passengers cheered and clapped. Some were crying hysterically, joyful that their lives had been saved.

"Please remain seated," Captain Petleruto said, "but you can safely remove your oxygen masks. You could have done so within minutes of the emergency hull's being activated, but we got a little busy in the cockpit for a while."

Annihilation of a Planet II

The riffling sound of masks being removed mixed with relieved laughter as passengers removed the masks. A collective, "Whew!" sounded throughout the compartment.

"The Coast Guard will be here shortly to tug us back close to shore," Petleruto continued. "From there, small rescue boats will be waiting to take you to land. You were understandably frightened, but I hope you will be able to look back on this as the ride of your life. You will be compensated for any luggage lost with the pieces of the craft that crashed into the ocean. To that end, there will be forms to fill out when we reach the airport, or forms will be mailed to your home if you choose to go straight there from landfall."

Various passengers raised their hands with questions about the forms, and the pilots answered calmly and politely. They were glad to have the passengers distracted from the fact that they were bobbing up and down in the Atlantic and the rescue team had not yet arrived. In the distance Petleruto saw the flag of a Coast Guard cutter and heard the sound of helicopters.

"If we can now all give a big hand to Lawrence, who saved the day for us."

In response to the wild cheering, clapping and whistling, Lawrence, still holding the puppy, stood and took a deep bow.

As helicopters hovered overhead, Coast Guard scuba divers descended on cables lowered from the aircraft. As soon as the divers reached the water, they began hitching long cables on improvised loops on the nylon capsule, preparing it to be tugged near the shore. Lawrence handed Sugarbear to Jerry and remained standing.

"Give thanks to your two brave pilots as well, ladies and gentlemen," Lawrence said, as people watched the divers through the clear shell of the inflated craft. "Under pressure for everyone's survival, they persevered!"

Now all the cheers and whistles went to the pilots, as everyone stood up from their chairs. Lawrence clapped with them. Looking at Jerry, he said, "It appears that Sugarbear does not belong to anyone on the plane. If no one claims him, maybe your parents will let you keep him." Both parents looked at Lawrence and agreed with a smile, mouthing a "thank you" to him. Sugarbear began to lick Jerry's cheeks, and the boy started to giggle, then laugh hysterically. Lawrence felt touched by the emotions of these humans, who watched in awe as the scuba divers departed via the same long cables on which they had descended, returning to the two helicopters hovering above. Coast Guard tugs were pulling the nylon craft at port and starboard, as well as from the bow. A fourth tug was aft. It was a complicated operation for a craft as large and buoyant as this one.

With a wave of his hand and a last, "Goodbye, everyone!" Lawrence vanished from the craft.

15
For Love

Caligula and Demetrius had landed safely on dry land by steering their parachute over the water toward shore. After disposing of their parachute they flagged down a sealander taxi. The sealander, which had been cruising along the low speed band of the Tesla belt, glided to a stop; the door opened and the seat rotated out. The two androids got in quickly, and the hatch closed.

"Where to?" the sealander asked.

"To New York City," Caligula directed, "but not by land. Take us by the ocean route to Hudson Bay, instead."

"Very good," the sealander replied, turning away from the Tesla belt and heading for the ocean.

Demetrius smiled. "They won't think of looking for us in Hudson Bay."

"You see, Demetrius, our artificial brain is far superior to man's three-pound piece of gray matter in his skull." His terrifying laughter filled the passenger compartment.

An hour later they had reached port. As Caligula put special coins into a payment slot in the passenger compartment, the seat swiveled out for the androids to debark.

"Thank you for your civic service!" Caligula called out as the sealander headed toward a nearby Tesla belt to resume its circuit around the outside edge.

Within a week Demetrius had gotten a new arm, stronger than the one he lost. In a matter of days they had taken the whole city block of the Empire State Building with their band of now 1,400 androids. They had taken hostages and spread them throughout the building as insurance against bombs or other explosive devices. Caligula was giving a speech as the U.S. Marines were engaging a small unit of the android forces in a firefight on the perimeter of the established block. The marines' goal was to take out Caligula and his second in command.

"In time we shall grow ever stronger!" Caligula declared. "With a larger army of androids, I shall march unimpeded to the Pentagon to alter the military droids and drones. I refuse to accept failure. What happened over the Atlantic Ocean was a setback, not a failure. It taught me that Lawrence is a true enemy. He is a very clever machine, and now that he knows where we are, we will wait for him and dispose of him for good before we march on to Washington, D.C."

Outside, the firefight was raging. There had been injuries on both sides. As night fell, laser bullets being shot from the guns of androids glowed red, coming out in staccatos from the machinegun-like weapons. Androids fell. So did marines. One of the marines was wrapping a tourniquet around his arm when Lawrence appeared.

"Can I be of any service?" Lawrence asked.

"Who are you?" The reply, a question, was surly and gruff.

"I am Lawrence B12 Android."

"Boy, we're glad to see you!" the marine said, his attitude changing immediately. "We've been waiting for your arrival. Caligula is inside the Empire State Building. He has taken up headquarters there with at least two dozen hostages. Coward. Hides himself behind innocent people."

Lawrence looked up at the tall skyscraper.

"If you can go in and take out him and his second in command, we can end this revolt tonight," the marine said, hope ringing in his voice.

Paul Linsdale approached the Imperial Estates, where he was supposed to find the mystery person to whom he would give Lawrence's letter. Slowly he got out of his sealander and walked toward the rose garden. Spotting the white gazebo in the distance, as Lawrence said he would, he also saw a woman seated there. She was gazing at the stars.

"Who goes there? Is that you, Lawrence?"

"No, I am Dr. Paul Linsdale, a family friend. He asked me to bring you this letter." Paul held up the letter; in his other hand he held the flower, the bird of paradise. Looking at her beautiful face, he saw her shy away from him. "Are you Lilah?"

"Yes, I am."

"You are an android, as well."

"Yes, designed for homecare."

"You are one of my father's earlier models. I recognize his work. This letter is for you from Lawrence. He wanted me to give it to you as a promise to keep your heart content until he comes back for you." Paul cleared his throat and shook his head. "I am confused as a scientist to say those words to you, but I find what's going on here to be incredibly fascinating!"

Lilah took the letter.

"May I hear what he has to say to you … for my scientific analysis?"

She nodded, acquiescing to his request. They sat down on a bench together in the gazebo. She carefully opened the envelope.

"Oh, also, he wants you to have this flower!" Linsdale said, silently cursing himself for being so absent-minded—a cliché that happened to be true of him.

Lilah took the flower and looked at the pretty colors. Drawing it close to her nose, she seemed to be able to smell the fragrance of the perfume scent it still held. Dr. Linsdale watched her every gesture, feeling greatly puzzled. He rubbed his chin with his hand, a look of dismay in his face. Placing the flower on her lap, Lilah unfolded the letter and began reading aloud in a soft voice.

"*Mio, amoré*. I will never forget the enchanting times we've had here in the garden, nor will I forget watching you one night gently caress back to sleep the two doves in their nest. Such memories allow me to write this poem to you.

One day Dove woke up in his nest,
only to find his love missing.
He flew around searching the world for her.
He became tired and asked God,
'Have you seen Love?'
God said to the dove,
"Go back to your nest and rest your tired wings."
Dove flew back only to find Love
back at the nest singing for his love.

Lilah looked up. "It is signed, 'I will always be your Valentine, Love.'"

Linsdale watched closely, noticing that the pupils of Lilah's eyes had become dilated with passion while reading the beautiful poem. Even he had been touched by the poem, and he wiped tears from his eyes. As he rubbed his fingers together to wipe away the moisture of the tears, he said, "How can this be? You two are machines. You cannot have feelings."

Before Lilah could respond, a call came in from Eli. A hologram of translucent cherubs erupted from his phone, flying around amid strains of violin music.

"Yes?" he said.

"Honey, it's time for you to take me to the hospital. The baby is coming!"

Linsdale jumped to his feet. "I'm going to be a father!" he yelled in excitement. "Lilah, I have to go. And Lawrence will be back for you soon."

"Congratulations!" she said.

For one more, brief moment Paul paused. "I considered myself a poet. Boy, my father was one great robotic engineer to create you two." Dashing away, he entered the sealander and commanded, "Take me home ASAP! Find the shortest route possible. The baby is coming!"

As if in a trance, Lilah slowly walked back to the house with flower and letter, which she had refolded and stuffed back into the envelope.

Lawrence brought the wounded marine to medics and hurried down farther to where a young lieutenant was in command. Laser machine gun tracers were lighting the skies, and sometimes direct hits on androids resulted in spectacular firework displays.

"Lieutenant, I am here to serve!" Lawrence announced.

"Who are you?" came the inevitable question.

"I am Lawrence Android B12."

"Thank God! We've been waiting for you! Caligula is on the 97th floor, according to our scanners picking up his frequency," the lieutenant said, pointing upward at the building.

With no more than a nod to the lieutenant, Lawrence disappeared. The officer turned away from the building to look back at Lawrence, but he was gone.

On the 97th floor, Lawrence stood looking around. Caligula was nowhere in sight, but he was still giving his speech, and Lawrence could hear him in the distance.

"I will capture the entire U.S.A., state by state. Then we will divide the forces of androids. I will lead most of you south to Mexico and South America. Demetrius, who is in the next room at the moment training a few of his troops, will take them and the rest of you north to Canada, then east to Europe. That's where we will join him. We will go together to the heart of all the continents—first to Israel and the Middle East, then into Africa, then to the Far East and Japan, and to Australia. The world will be ours!"

As Caligula laughed uproariously in front of his army of droids, he continued to speak in an upbeat manner. "The American Henry Adams was a man before his time. In 1862 he wrote, 'One day science will be the master of men. The engines he will have invented will be beyond his strength to control, and he will have no choice but to blow up the world.' I say to you, my soldiers, we will take control and enslave humans to work for us. We won't let them destroy the earth!"

Caligula's sinister laugh ricocheted down the hallway, raising the hair at the back of the necks of the hostages in nearby rooms. At that moment, Lawrence burst into the room where Demetrius stood with some 90 androids geared up to destroy any humans in their path. Demetrious turned to see Lawrence.

"We've been expecting you, Lawrence," Demetrius said, clinching his fists. "As you can see, I have another arm, and this one is better than the one you ripped out. Now we will rip you apart from limb to limb. You had your chance to join us. You stand there looking like a rock! But where is the freakin' granite inside?"

With those words Demetrius nodded to two giant androids with eye scopes from the back of their heads to front, allowing them to see 360 degrees at all times. They never had to turn their heads.

They grabbed Lawrence from the back and held him like a ramming cage, ramming his head through concrete walls, leaving holes in the walls. Next the giants, which had been designed for demolition work, threw Lawrence through a steel wall, and the hostages in the adjoining room screamed in fright.

Annihilation of a Planet II

Lawrence, dazed, knew his circuits were losing power, and he felt weak. Plaster dust covered his outer shell, and his uniform was in shreds, leaving only his torn pants still on.

The noise had interrupted Caligula's rant, and he rushed out of his chamber to see what all the commotion was about. Demetrius looked at his leader and grinned, saying, "Under that pile of steel and rock debris lies the great Lawrence! We will now dismantle him, piece by piece." Demetrius looked at his gigantic stewards. "Finish him off!"

The giants lumbered toward Lawrence as Caligula and Demetrius watched with anticipation.

Under the crumbled wreckage Lawrence silently prayed, *God, I ask of you, let me be the artificial light to help mankind until the true light of God, your Son, returns! I bear the strength of the mighty Samson, but I ask you to give me the intense electrifying energy of the Ultimate Warrior! Unleash my might!*

As the two ten-foot androids approached the rubble, needing to dig Lawrence out before they could dismantle him, the other androids were waiting with interest, each one hoping to get a piece of the world-famous savior. As the last piece of rubble was removed, Lawrence felt a surge of energy intensifying his normal, magnificent strength. He leapt upward and grabbed the right arm of each of the giant androids, smashing their bodies together in mid-air three times. As they broke apart into pieces, Lawrence continued to hold onto the right arms, using them to take out a few other robots standing nearby, decapitating some of them in a shower of sparks.

The army of androids from the other room had surged in to protect Caligula. Lawrence looked at the one thousand robots, and he remembered what the astronaut captain had said on the tarmac when they returned from Mars. It seemed to be something humans said when they were facing danger courageously. This situation seemed appropriate, and he shouted, "Let's rock!" as he stood tall and proud.

If there had been no hostages, he would have used his sonic clap to take care of them all in one gesture, but he knew that move would harm the hostages irreparably. He downloaded the old rock 'n' roll Van Halen track, "Eruption," with its high frequency electric guitar sound. Turning the sound up, Lawrence saw the androids hunch over, trying to close off their hearing receptors, unable to think clearly enough to fight. Windows began to burst and shatter, and the people down below held their ears tightly. Lawrence looked up toward the ceiling and began to pound his chest with his fists, in imitation of the Ultimate Warrior.

Demetrius yelled, "Get him! Now!"

Seeing a long cable wire about three inches in diameter, Lawrence picked it up and started shaking it up and down wildly, pulling and twisting it back and forth. Finally it snapped loose, and Lawrence whipped it around to take out dozens of androids at a time as they charged him.

Annihilation of a Planet II

"Demetrius!" Caligula shouted. "Do something! Are you going to let this bastard take you again?"

Demetrius charged, and with one single blow Lawrence knocked off the rebel's head. Catching the head and throwing it away from himself in a dismissive gesture, Lawrence strode toward Caligula. Lawrence's arms rotated like helicopter blades, snapping off heads and arms of androids as he went. Caligula, whose design had been altered to make him an imitation of Lawrence, was nothing like the real thing. The would-be emperor had run out onto the ledge through a broken window, and he was holding tightly onto the skyscraper. Lawrence grabbed his weak twin by the shoulder and tried to transport with him, but the transporting device did not work. It had been damaged when the giants shoved him so many times through the walls.

Suddenly Caligula began fighting back. "Unhand me! Now!" he yelled.

In the struggle, both androids lost their footing on the ledge, and they went spiraling downward together. To Lawrence, time seemed to slow down, as though in suspended animation, and his expression was lifeless.

"Let me go!" Caligula yelled. "We can save ourselves by grabbing onto the building if you'll just let me go!"

Lawrence knew if he let Caligula go he could get away again. Lawrence was not going to take the chance. As he bear-hugged the rebel leader tightly, the look-alike robots continued to fall backward, head first.

As they plunged to certain destruction, Lawrence recalled the Titanic, the "unsinkable ship" that struck an iceberg. Now he, Lawrence, was like the Titanic, heretofore indestructible, but the Empire State building was his iceberg. He recalled how those famously brave musicians kept playing on that cold night to warm the hearts of the passengers—those who would perish and those who would get on lifeboats hoping they would be saved and live to tell the story.

"This is our iceberg," Lawrence said calmly to Caligula, who looked back at him in confusion. "Mankind must live. He is a gift from God that will reach out into the far universe. Perhaps our deaths will awaken in man the desire for peace and a commitment to care for the planet."

Caligula made one last, mighty effort to get away, but Lawrence had a death grip on his twin. Against the backdrop of stars glimpsed between buildings, Lawrence pictured himself and the friends he had made along the way of his artificial life—his first friend, Larf, the talking ape; Brian and Austin at the grand ball, fraternizing with the women there; the cute face of the Brazilian girl, Estrella, kissing him on the cheeks ("You're my Prince Perfect"); his first client, Ellen, who started him on this great adventure to find love, the strongest force in the Universe.

Obliterating for a moment Lawrence's memories, a camera drone locked onto the falling androids. It

Annihilation of a Planet II

caught Caligula's question, "Why, Lawrence? Why must you rebel against your own kind?"

And the camera's recorder also picked up Lawrence's answer: "There was once a boy," Lawrence said, smiling and thinking of Jerry giggling as Sugarbear licked him in the face. "And once there was a cry, a desperate cry from the moon to save the Earth, and in that cry of the moon, there was hope, and love was in that hope. For that reason there will be another boy ... greater than his father ... greater even than his grandfather. He will answer that cry, bringing hope and love to all."

Now to Lawrence's artificial brain the warm, smiling face of Lilah came, giving him a passionate kiss. They were in the garden looking up at the stars, glimmering with soft white lights.

"I did it for the"—he paused with a smile, with a look of fulfillment in his quest for love—"for the power and the glory ... of love!"

The two man-made machines, one that stood for good and the other that aimed for the destruction of man, made sudden impact with the street. They made a crater the size of a sealander bus, and clusters of black smoke spewed upward, sending the camera drone flying away along with the detritus. When it cleared, the marines shone a light into the crater. The lieutenant, looking down into the large pit, saw the broken fragments of the androids, scattered together in a million pieces. It was the end of an era.

Global News Network, like every other network station in the world, was covering the event. "This is all we have of the great Lawrence," a voice over said, as a drone camera flew into the pit to get a close-up of Lawrence's chin and half of his face still intact, with his eye closed. The camera on the drone captured an image of part of another face—it, too was a right side. The eye was also closed.

"Two identical half faces," the voice continued. "In repose they look the same, but one stood for evil, while the other was only good. What could have made the difference? One was created by the father, the other by the son. Perhaps the difference lay in the purpose behind the construction. Who can say? At this stage of invention of artificial intelligence, man must take great care to avoid bringing Mary Shelley's monster to life in the form of a machine."

A two-minute collage of Lawrence's life, featuring scenes of his early life as a caregiver, leaving with the Cybernauts 30 years previously, hanging from the death pole on Mars, his return from Mars in Project Yu Yan, his sighting in the Middle East and in Brazil in the confrontation with the contractors, and finally his final resting place outside the Empire State Building.

A GNN camera turned back to the co-anchors, Charles Doherty and Angela Barry, who continued to stare silently at their monitors for a full five seconds. Uncharacteristically, Charles had a tear in his eye, and as Angela glanced over at him, she felt her heart leap to her throat, and she placed a hand there. She had never known Charles to be touched by anything

Annihilation of a Planet II

romantic. He had always been so stern and self-possessed, never letting anything get to him. Yet Lawrence's words somehow had moved him.

"Charles? Are you all right?"

"Never better, Angela." He looked down and cleared his throat. "Please come around in front of the news desk."

"What?"

"No talking." He held out his hand to her. "Please."

She put her hand in his, and they walked together to the front of the news desk, stepping over the cables that snaked in front of it. One camera stayed on them as Charles got down on one knee.

"Lawrence showed me the meaning of life ... and love, today, Angela. Will you marry me?"

Angela put her hands to her face and peered out through her fingers. "Charles? Is this really you?"

"No one else."

"You are the man I've been searching for under that tough exterior." She reached down to pull him up. "Yes, Charles. As long as you remember this day and allow me to see this sweetness in you, I will be your wife."

People on the set broke out in cheers and applause as the happy couple kissed.

"We now return to our regular programming," declared the voice that had accompanied the collage of Lawrence's life.

Brian and Austin, both of them with sleeves rolled up and sorting through papers and electronic messages, were busy making arrangements with adoption agencies around the world for the Brazilian street children—not only the seventeen Lawrence had rescued, but also many others who continued to barely exist each day in fear for their lives.

"Oh, man! Let's take a break," Brian said. "I'm tired of reading and hearing excuses from some of these agencies.

"But the good news is we've placed nearly a hundred children," Austin said.

"Yes, and you're personally placing two of them yourself, my friend," Brian said. "I think you're right in keeping it secret till after the election. The opposing party would be bound to smear you for using the adoption to create sympathy for yourself."

"Or not." Austin grinned. "I already feel toward the children as a father would, and my wife is totally in love with Artie and Estrella."

"That little Estrella is going to have you wrapped around her pinkie finger," Brian said with a laugh as he picked up a remote and clicked on the TV set. Both men watched in horror as the drone camera followed the two Lawrences onto the pavement and into the pit. Without a word between them, Brian and Austin watched the live feed, and when the last picture of the Lawrence collage faded, Brian clicked it off.

Tears ran down their faces, and they turned and hugged each other.

Annihilation of a Planet II

"Valor!" whispered Brian.

"Virtue!" Austin whispered back.

Carrying the old man's slippers in her hand, Lilah came into the retired general's room as he watched one of his favorite old classic TV shows. She dropped the slippers and stopped dead still when the show was interrupted.

"This is Global News Network with late-breaking news. The world renowned android Lawrence was destroyed just hours ago when he saved the world once again. The android revolt is over, and it was Lawrence who saved us all."

Across the screen came scenes of U.S. Marines, aiming their laser guns at what was left of the rebel androids, which were being pushed into a truck that would take them to be scrapped.

Lilah stood like a statue as she watched the screen showing pieces of her beloved Lawrence in the concrete detritus along with what was left of his evil twin. As she watched the collage of his life, she knew it would not include anything about her. That secret would be held in her artificial mind forever.

She bent to pick up the old general's slippers and quietly put them on his feet.

"Now that my feet are nice and warm and that silly business with a robot revolt is over, maybe I can enjoy my show," he said. "Wait. What's this nonsense?"

"It seems that Mr. Doherty is proposing to Ms. Barry. Oh, isn't that sweet?" Lilah said. "I think Lawrence played Cupid in one of his last acts on earth.

Mr. Carter harrumphed, and a frown creased his forehead.

Finally came the announcement, "We now return to our regular programming."

"Anything else, Mr. Carter?"

"I'm good."

As she walked toward the door to leave, she heard the sound of someone Lawrence had enjoyed pretending to be. General Carter was watching an old wrestling show that featured a wrestler called the Ultimate Warrior. When his entry music came on, Lilah paused to watch, saw him running down the aisle with intense energy, electrifying the crowd and shaking the ropes wildly, running and bouncing off the ropes, then standing at the top turn buckle. The announcer yelled out his name.

"It's the Ultimate … Warrior!"

As the painted face of the wrestler appeared, Mr. Carter wriggled in his chair with excitement. The muscular performer, wearing his championship belt, moved his arms around so that the neon-colored strings tied to his elbows whipped around his strong arms. When he pounded his chest and roared like a lion, Mr. Carter yelled, "Boy! He's going to devour his opponent!"

Annihilation of a Planet II

Lilah took the love poem from her pocket and held it where a heart would be if she had been given one. Staring into the distance, she remembered Lawrence's sweet words, *"Um beijo para a meu caracão"*—a kiss to my heart. She whispered softly, "You will always be my Valentine ... to the end of time."

"It's a healthy, eight-pound boy!" the doctor said as he handed the baby to Eli. Paul had been informed of the destruction of Lawrence during Eli's labor at the hospital. Linsdale was a bundle of ambivalent feelings—sorrow over the demise of his father's great creation and delight in the birth of his own son. Paul took his newborn child into his arms and stood by his wife's side.

"May we register his name, Dr. Linsdale?" a nurse asked. "What have you and your wife decided to name him?"

"We have decided to name him Lawrence Love Linsdale!" Paul declared, as Eli lay smiling up at father and son. "The name will be a reminder of Lawrence B12's last words, captured by the camera drone and beamed around the world. He sacrificed himself for the glory of love."

The hospital personnel were touched by this gesture, and tears shimmered in every eye. They would never forget this day, when a manmade machine helped the world become a better, safer place to live.

On the day a special baby was born, people all over the world would have seared into their memory exactly where they were the day an android named Lawrence chose destruction for himself in exchange for saving humankind. Would they use that salvation to care for the planet he seemed to love? That is the question.

The End.

Annihilation of a Planet II

"Through The Ages." History has shown that life measures not someone's footsteps, but the extraordinary footprints they have left behind. Towards the goodwill for mankind.

Antonion Borges